MAR 29 '95

THE FABER BOOK OF
CONTEMPORARY LATIN AMERICAN
SHORT STORIES

ff

The Faber Book of
CONTEMPORARY LATIN AMERICAN SHORT STORIES

Edited by Nick Caistor

faber and faber
LONDON · BOSTON

First published in 1989
by Faber and Faber Limited
3 Queen Square London WC1N 3AU
This paperback edition first published in 1990

Photoset by Parker Typesetting Service Leicester
Printed in Great Britain by
Richard Clay Ltd Bungay Suffolk
All rights reserved

*A CIP record for this book is available
from the British Library*
ISBN 0-571-15360-7

For Rachel, Anna and Lulu

Contents

Acknowledgements

The editor and publishers would like to thank the following for permission to use the stories in this volume: Daniel Moyano and *Index on Censorship* for 'Aunt Lila'; the editors of the *Journal of Literary Translation* for 'Uncle Facundo' by Isidoro Blaisten; North Point Press for 'Up Among the Eagles' by Luisa Valenzuela from *Open Door*, 1988; João Ubaldo Ribeiro for 'Alaindelon de la Patrie'; Agencia Literaria Latinoamericana for 'Peace and War' by Moacyr Scliar from *Olho Enigmatico*, Editora Guanabara, 1986; Agencia literaria Carmen Balcells for 'The Judge's Wife' by Isabel Allende; Reinaldo Arenas for 'Adiós a Mama'; Arturo Arias and *Index on Censorship* for 'Woman in the Middle'; Four Walls Eight Windows, and Peter Owen Publishers for 'The Proof' by Rodrigo Rey Rosa; Jesús Gardea for 'Martina's Wardrobe'; María Luisa Puga and Martín Casillas Editores for 'The Trip' from *Accidentes*, 1981; Readers International for 'Saint Nikolaus' by Sergio Ramírez from *Stories*, 1986; Agencia Literaria Latinoamericana for 'Chicken for Three' by Fernando Silva, from *Cuentos*, Editorial Nueva Nicaragua, 1985; Editorial Araverá for 'Under Orders' by Helio Vera, from *Angola y otros cuentos*, 1984; Agencia Literaria Carmen Balcells for 'Anorexia With Scissors' by Alfredo Bryce Echenique from *Magdalena Peruana y otros cuentos*, Plaza & Janes, 1986; Arte Publico Press for 'The Rites' by Rolando Hinojosa from *Rites and Witnesses*, 1982; Eduardo Galeano for 'The Rest is Lies' from *Contraseña*, Ediciones del Sol, 1985; Agencia Literaria Carmen Balcells and *Index on Censorship* for 'Presence' by Juan Carlos Onetti; Cristina Peri Rossi for 'The Museum of Vain Endeavours'; Marcha Editores, Mexico, for 'The Game' by Luis Britto García, from *Novísimos narradores hispanoamericanos en Marcha*, 1981.

Introduction

Readers in Britain and the United States started to appreciate
Latin American fiction in the late 1960s and early 1970s. They
realized that here was another part of the world producing a
distinctive body of work, an exciting aesthetic reflection on an
area that was in itself exotic and challenging. Events in Latin
America – a revolution in Cuba, Che Guevara preaching
rebellion throughout the subcontinent, attempts in Chile to
find a path to socialism – were paralleled by a literature that
also suggested exciting new discoveries were at hand.

Latin American literature became the equivalent of the
Amazon rain-forest, providing oxygen for the stale literary
lungs of the developed world of Europe and the United
States. Since the sixteenth century, Latin America has been
the site for El Dorado, a place of untold riches; now literature
added a new dimension to the fabulous myth.

Short stories were central to these riches. Though the way
Latin American fiction was 'discovered' outside the subcontinent obscured the genuine differences in talents as diverse
as Borges, Rulfo, Carpentier, García Márquez or Cortázar, it
was plain they were all using the short story as a vital part of
their armoury as they explored and tried to make sense of the
world around them.

The rush for Latin American literary gold led to the works
being presented as though they had been written at one and
the same time, and as if the region were a homogeneous
whole with similar concerns and a shared literary tradition.
Literary generations did not exist, it seemed, and any sense
of development or active interplay with a national heritage
was obscured. In fact, these writers came from diverse cul-
tural backgrounds and the work was produced over a period
of thirty years or more.

This upsurge in Latin American literature is by no means

over. Writers have continued to work after the 'boom' just as they did before it. For the younger generation, the internationally acclaimed authors are there to be assimilated, to argue with, to measure up to, and move beyond.

In this anthology I want to convey a sense of how twenty contemporary Latin American writers have been doing just that over the past ten years. During this time, the short story has continued to play a key role in the region's literature. In part this is due to the strength of the tradition established by earlier generations; in part it is because short stories are still relatively easy to get published, even in the economic chaos characteristic of the past decade. To give some sense of literary context, I have used the countries the stories were written in to structure the anthology. I have also chosen one story written by a Chicano writer living in the United States, as a reminder that the Hispanic presence there is already creating a literary space for itself.

Though the majority of writers included are of the younger generation, for me the collection is ushered in by a writer now in his eightieth year. The Uruguayan Juan Carlos Onetti, author of the short story 'Presence', is one of the 'boom' generation who saw his peers gain recognition outside Latin America but went largely unrecognized himself, perhaps because his work in no way fitted in with what quickly came to be a stereotyped view of the region's literary production. Onetti has, however, been a major influence for the next generation of Latin American writers, both in his use of language and the range of feeling explored. 'Presence' is also significant for the circumstances in which it was written. Onetti, then in his sixties, happened to be a member of a literary jury which awarded a prize to a short story which the military authorities in Uruguay found offensive. Taken into custody and roughed up, Onetti left for Spain immediately he was released, and has never returned.

'Presence', one of the first stories written by Onetti in exile, is an attempt, known to be a cruel illusion from the outset, to retain links with all that has been lost. This sense of dispossession is strong in many of the writers represented here, who, from Guatemala in the north to Argentina and Chile in the south, have had to come to terms with political violence

INTRODUCTION

and social disruption. Exile has been a fact of life for many writers. Apart from Onetti, out of the twenty authors in this anthology, Daniel Moyano, Eduardo Galeano, Arturo Arias, Reinaldo Arenas and Cristina Peri Rossi have been forced to leave their home countries. Isabel Allende, Luisa Valenzuela, and Alfredo Bryce Echenique have also felt it impossible to live and thrive as writers in their own lands.

This situation makes the affirmation at the heart of all writing even more important. It also makes the short story perhaps the most adequate vehicle for capturing the urgency of leaving some record of events and emotions that is free from the distorted messages of politics and official history. This is what leads Luisa Valenzuela to conclude, in the preface to her latest book of short stories: 'I must hurry now, and write other stories: it is the only way I know of jamming a foot in the door so it won't slam in our faces.' (*Open Door*, North Point Press, San Francisco, 1988)

This sense of urgency also pervades the work of those short-story writers who look back on their subcontinent's history, trying to discover in it the roots of violence and the origin of the feeling of dispossession they experience, even in their own lands. But there is also the triumphant assertion of a story like Eduardo Galeano's 'The Rest is Lies', which insists that love is a force that will not succumb to death, and is as much a response to the thousands of forced disappearances which have occurred in the subcontinent in recent years as it is a speculation on the region's prehistory.

A different kind of urgency emerges in those writers who are not so concerned with the region's history or with its jungles, but who instead explore life in the great modern cities of Latin America. They try to convey the frenetic pace and confusion of daily existence in places like Mexico City, Buenos Aires, São Paulo, Rio de Janeiro or Lima. Rapid dialogue and humour are more important to them than any magic or myths.

The level of myth will not be denied though, and several of the stories in the anthology reflect the continuing efforts of writers throughout the region to arrive at fables that are timeless and irrefutable. Working within a vein opened up by a previous generation, they invent new circumstances and symbols which continue to ring true.

What I have tried to convey in this anthology is an idea of the possibilities that new Latin American writers have found in the short story over the last uneasy decade. In choosing the pieces I have followed much the same process as the one used by short-story writers themselves: I have tried to suggest a whole vibrant world which continues beyond the few pages at my disposal. I hope others will be convinced, as I am, that the Latin American short story of the 1980s is adventurous and rewarding.

Nick Caistor
London
February 1989

ARGENTINA

Uncle Facundo

ISIDORO BLAISTEN

To give you some idea what my family was like before we dispatched Uncle Facundo – or, rather, before Uncle Facundo arrived – I'm going to let you in on the things each of us used to say.

Mother said: Dogs know when their master's going to die. Nothing's worse than operating when there's fever. Penicillin eats up the red blood cells. *She said*, Kids get dehydrated in the summer. Boys go more for their mothers and girls their fathers. Children from broken homes are always sad. Jewish doctors are the best. *She said*, The worst child's always the one the mother loves best. Those who have most spend least and may even be poor. And to think she was already carrying the cancer around inside her. *She said*, Wallpaper attracts bugs. People used to die of the flu once.

Father said: Swimming's the perfect sport. The cold was what lost the Germans the war in Russia. Soldiers and sailors all wear horns (travelling salesmen too). Actually the best thing for shaving is the straight razor. Nothing like a good glass of red wine in winter and a nice beer in summer. Thin ones are the best in bed. Never chill a red wine. Turkish tobacco's healthier than Virginia. No doctor operates on his own wife. At the end of the day all the working man wants is his fried steak and his glass of wine. Money in the bank and they're looking for charity. Thieves – I'd cut off their hands and hang them in the Plaza de Mayo. Horse manure, that's the best fertilizer. The real money's in the land. Your barbecue has to be eaten on your feet. Country people don't know what problems are: an ear of corn, a couple of eggs, kill a chicken, and they're all set.

My sister said: There's nothing nicer than going to the movies when it rains. A bird on its own dies of sadness. People with fair skins burn right away, people with dark don't. They go from man to man and after that . . . I hate pictures that make you cry. Me, I could go on learning for ever. Not like some who get married in white. My principal, I don't know why she insists on the global method.

I said: No two ways about it, you have to take your hat off to German industry. The Japanese – they'll stab you in the back every time. Swimming builds up weak muscles. Guys with chips on their shoulder cool off fast. Until I graduate – no girls. For me, politics should be kept out of the classroom.

That's how my family was until Uncle Facundo arrived. Father worked for the railway in the freight office at Retiro Station. He got up every morning at five, had his *maté* while he read *Clarín* from front to back, then walked the seven blocks to Saavedra Station. Mother looked after the house, watered the plants, and watched television. My sister's hobby was pyrography. She was a schoolteacher and was studying to be a social worker.

I studied economics and had a job in the accounts department at Casimires Bonplart, the textile company.

When we were kids, I remember Mother and Father always talking about Uncle Facundo in low voices. But whenever my sister or I came near they always broke off their conversation.

During the summer, after supper, Father would carry Mother's wicker chair outside, then the low chair for himself, the Viennese chair (which I rocked in) for me, and the folding chair for my sister.

On those nights, it invariably happened that Father would say something about the progress of the wall going up in our back garden, then tell us again about the time his letter was published in *Clarín*, whereupon Mother – I don't know why – would chime in about Uncle Facundo.

Uncle Facundo was Mother and Aunt Fermina's brother. Father didn't know him and we didn't either. By the time Mother and Father were going out together, Uncle Facundo had already disappeared. When we were old enough to understand any of this, Mother told us Uncle Facundo had got married in Casilda, in the Province of Santa Fe, that his wife had died mysteriously, and that all the gossips (and Aunt Fermina) were saying Uncle Facundo had killed her.

Uncle Facundo was the black sheep of Mother's family.

Aunt Fermina said that as far as she was concerned she didn't have a brother and that it was his fault that our grandmother had died of a broken heart.

One day there was a telegram from Uncle Facundo. 'Dear Family,' it read. 'Arriving Friday the 10th, Posadas international train.'

Father was dead against his staying with us, but Mother said that he was her brother after all, and that the poor boy must be feeling very lonely, and that if he didn't want to stay with Aunt Fermina and was choosing our house instead there must have been a good reason for it.

Anyway, that Friday night, at 11.45, we were all there at Chacarita Station. The train was running about two hours late, and while we waited in the station café an argument started up.

Uncle Facundo was a good-for-nothing, Father said, but he was always welcome for a few days. However, in no way was he to get the idea that Father was going to support him for the rest of his life. Mother and my sister said it was bad enough for someone to be hanging from the edge of a cliff without others having to trample on his fingers instead of helping him. I didn't say anything. Just then the train came in.

We had a bit of a time finding Uncle Facundo. Since Mother was the only one who knew him, we kept looking at her face. At last she spotted him. He was standing against a column, clutching a package the size of a shoebox.

The moment I laid eyes on him I felt I'd known Uncle Facundo all my life. That was the way he made you feel. He lifted Mother off her feet, kissed her, gave Father a big hug that made him cough, picked up Angelita like a bride, put a hand on my shoulder and, without saying a word, stared at me as if I were his accomplice.

'Come on!' he exclaimed. 'Let's have a drink. I want to show you a few things.'

Father said they should first claim Uncle Facundo's baggage. But apart from the shoebox Uncle Facundo had no baggage.

In the café he ordered white wine for everyone. Mother and Father looked at each other. Except for Father (a drop or two with lots of soda), none of us drank wine. But my sister, who was in the clouds, was desperate to see what Uncle Facundo had brought; as a matter of fact, we were all intrigued. We drank our wine and even had a second round. Mother was unrecognizable and kept laughing loudly, especially when Uncle Facundo lifted the top off the box and gave her a Paraguayan shawl of *ñandutí* lace made by Indian women. It was beautiful and its colours striking. It was something Mother had always wanted.

That night Uncle Facundo won us over. He made us each gifts of things we had always longed for. Father got a box of Havana cigars. Havana Havanas. The best and most expensive, not those smelly stogies his friend Michelini brought him from Brazil. Real Havanas.

My sister got a ring and matching necklace. The links fitted into one another, becoming smaller or larger, and when the whole thing was clasped together an aquamarine hung between the gold and silver sections. My sister jumped for joy and gave him a kiss.

When he handed me a knife and I saw it had a Solingen blade with the little tree brand on it, I think I felt sick. It had a gold-inlaid silver sheath and handle, and was beautifully worked. I never saw another like it.

We had a final round of wine. Father paid, and we all went home in a taxi. That night, except for Uncle Facundo, none of us slept a wink.

That was the first battle Uncle Facundo won over us. I can't imagine what he got out of it, but then I can't imagine what we got out of killing him either. What did Mother get out of suffocating him with a pillow? What did Father get out of strangling him, or me out of sticking the knife he gave me between his breastbone and his heart while my sister slashed his wrists with a razor blade?

No, it didn't do any good at all. Uncle Facundo's still there, embedded in the garden wall, on his side like a swimmer, maybe shrivelled up or maybe not. Maybe where his body was is just a hollow now, while every day the sun hardens the mortar, and Uncle Facundo's still there. But that happened later, much later, when we had no choice but to kill him.

The day after that memorable night, Uncle Facundo was

the first one out of bed. This too was memorable, because from that time on, until he met his end (and then more than ever), it always took for ever to get him up.

It was on Saturday, and Uncle Facundo went into the back garden, where, beside the wall that was to become his tomb, he found some empty bitumen cans and tools. With these he built Mother a little set of corner shelves, and afterwards went and woke her up with a cup of *maté*.

Around noon, when we were all up and saw what Uncle Facundo had made, we were amazed by his handiwork. That's when he told us that real work was what you did with your hands, and all the rest – figures and paperwork – was a sham and pussy-footing.

Lunch that day was a celebration. Uncle Facundo told us all about how he'd harvested rice in Entre Ríos and worked on cattle ranches in Corrientes. But his funniest story was about the time he was a gravedigger in Casilda. It was at this point he sent my sister to buy a couple more bottles of wine. Later, her eyes shining, Mother suggested we play the lottery, but Uncle Facundo said poker was a lot more fun, and we all stared at each other because none of us knew the game and besides there was the problem of the cards.

Mother asked what cards you needed for poker. Uncle Facundo explained, and she went off to ransack a cupboard. Back she came with an unopened box containing a set of draughts, a small top with numbers on it, two packs of cards, and chips. She had bought these in a sale at Gath & Chaves.

'Are these the right cards?' she asked, tearing off the cellophane wrapper. Luckily they were, Uncle Facundo taught us to play, and poker became the most wonderful, exciting game any of us had ever played. At first the chips weren't worth anything, then we made them ten pesos, then fifty, then a hundred. Father sent my sister to get another two bottles of wine, but Uncle Facundo said two of cheap rum would be better. Just as Angelita was on her way out, Aunt Fermina popped in.

When Aunt Fermina saw what was on the table she almost died. She didn't even say hello to my uncle after all those years. Instead, she insulted him, calling him everything under the sun. Mother, who seemed half drunk, rushed to his defence. Father absentmindedly shook his head, saying, 'Calm down, everybody, calm down.'

But suddenly Father got to his feet, reached across the table, and gave my sister a slap, upsetting everything – chips, cards, money.

'What are you waiting for, stupid?' he exploded. 'Go and get the rum right away.'

It was the first time in my life I'd seen my father raise a hand against my sister.

Angelita ran off to the corner shop, while Uncle Facundo went out into the garden for a smoke. He stood there by the back wall, looking up at the stars that were just beginning to come out.

Now that I think about it, it seemed that Uncle Facundo had a soft spot for that wall, where he's now sealed up behind brick, his mouth and eyes full of cement, although maybe there's nothing left but the air around his bones. You'd have to tap the wall to find out.

Well, Aunt Fermina finally left, and at first nobody was hungry, but after a while Uncle Facundo began cracking jokes. He sent my sister for two more bottles of wine and showed Mother how to cook *saltimbocca alla romana*. We ate like kings, drank the two bottles of rum, and went on playing poker till six in the morning.

The next day the neighbours complained, and Father, who missed work for the first time in his life, wanted to hit Michelini.

And that's how it all began. Every Saturday and Sunday, Father and Uncle Facundo went to the racetrack. Mother handed them the family savings to bet with.

Angelita brought home all her schoolteacher friends, and Uncle Facundo taught them to dance the tango and then got them into bed. Mother came unstuck and went out every night with a young poet. Uncle Facundo said that was good, it was healthy, it was life, that you had to grab life with both hands, that beauty and pornography should go hand in hand, and that people's greatest problem when there were no wars was boredom. That's why, he said, your neighbours spent their lives hanging out of their windows living other people's lives; gossip was a sort of frustrated romanticism, and people devoured crime or erotic magazines because that's what they needed, because they found life in them, because real life is a wash-out.

I brought my classmates home so that they could hear the things Uncle Facundo said.

Up to this point things could have gone well. Father, who'd never had it in him to harm a fly even, had beaten up almost all our neighbours, and at first they came around only out of respect for him, but soon they became fixtures, following him around and admiring his paintings.

Father had discovered his 'hidden vocation', as Uncle Facundo called it, and his pictures hung all over the house. Michelini was often there looking at them for hours on end. Sometimes his eyes misted over, he'd give Father a pat on the back, and leave without a word.

I had changed; I was aware of my own personal magnetism. So were the girls in my class. They adored me and came home with me.

We all lived life to the full. There wasn't a minute or a hair-space we had to worry about filling in. It was as if everything was greased with life. Every night there was dancing, poker, and sitting at Uncle Facundo's feet. Mother read the young poet's latest work; Father painted, studied the racing form, and got into rows. We squeezed life for every drop it held.

But my sister took to playing the leftist intellectual, and this was where her conscience came into play. First it was the dehumanizing effect of bourgeois sensuality, then she moved on to the dialogue between Catholics and Marxists. All Father wanted to do was hit her. That's when Angelita and Aunt Fermina joined forces.

Aunt Fermina liked to chew over pet hatreds. From the time Uncle Facundo appeared on the scene, she had been around to preach on two or three occasions, but she was afraid of Father, who wanted to hit her every time he laid eyes on her. Here was her big chance now.

The first thing Aunt Fermina did, abetted by my sister, was to slip into the house one Sunday while we were still asleep and destroy every last one of Father's paintings with a palette knife.

Poor Father! It was the portrait of Dorian Gray all over again. I remember the way he looked when he saw the slashed canvases, the tubes of paint squeezed out, the trampled stretchers. He didn't say a word. But the next morning, Monday, he was his old self again. He was up at five, had his *maté*, read *Clarín* from front to back, and that evening carried his low chair outside. Meanwhile, indoors, the rest of us were dancing, playing poker, or listening to the young poet's poems.

It was Father's turn to wake up now, and he threw in with my sister and Aunt Fermina. Anyway, even before Aunt Fermina took the next step, before she converted me (though Mother was the last to give in, she was the one who, when she suffocated Uncle Facundo with the pillow, showed the most passion), even before Father was won over by Aunt Fermina, I mean, something had begun to break down, something that made things easier for Aunt Fermina. It was seeing Father walking around like a zombie, completely changed, explaining that the cold was what lost the Germans the war in Russia, while those of us on Uncle Facundo's side were still living life to the hilt.

It wasn't hard for Aunt Fermina to win me over. By then life was going downhill. Mother, however, proved a hard nut to crack. She was the young poet's lover (he saw in her, according to Uncle Facundo, both mother and woman). The boy was crazy about Mother, and he wrote her some wonderful poems. But Mother was alone.

Then Aunt Fermina made a breakthrough. She snatched Mother aside and presented her with the dilemma. 'You're the only one left,' my aunt said. 'Either we kill Facundo or your poet.'

Love won. That night we decided to kill Uncle Facundo. We found him asleep with an unforgettable smile on his face. Father strangled him, and I stabbed him between his breastbone and his heart. My sister slashed his wrists with a razor blade. The whole thing had been organized by Aunt Fermina. Tearing Mother away had been the only difficult part. She didn't want to withdraw the pillow from Uncle Facundo's face. We propped him on his side and built the wall up around him. And that's the whole story.

But now that Uncle Facundo's there, a piece of the wall for ever and calcifying under the sun, I can't help looking at that corner of the garden with a touch of sadness – above all on summer nights, when Father carries Mother's wicker chair outside, then the low chair for himself, the Viennese chair (which I rock in) for me, and the folding chair for my sister, and Mother says, 'Dogs know when their master's going to die,' and Father says, 'The real money's in the land,' and my sister says, 'My principal, I don't know why she insists on the global method,' and I say, 'The Japanese – they'll stab you in the back every time.'

Translated by Cynthia Ventura

Aunt Lila

DANIEL MOYANO

Poor Aunt Lila! So tall, such an old maid in her white dress. The nimblest fingers in the hills had worked at its pleats to shape it like a swaying bell every afternoon when Aunt Lila called out to us from the veranda: Boys, stop playing with that ball, come in and wash your hands, scrub your knees, wipe your nose, it's time to pray. So thickly pleated was her dress that she could swirl it in any direction without ever revealing her knees; there were always more folds, even when she plucked the tip of the skirt and lifted it shoulder high like a peacock, or raised both hands above her head so that the bell closed round like a huge rosette. When she danced, it was a great sweep of material, its folds eddying out like the whirlpool where Uncle Jacinto had drowned. Then there was all its lace and embroidery: the brightly coloured threads shaped into two big butterflies over the bosom, the smaller ones on the sleeves, where yellow ribbons enclosed her wrists. Aunt Lila was one huge white mass.

Boys, today we're going to Cosquín to see Uncle Emilio. Mind you behave, don't take your catapults, don't go killing any pigeons or catching any finches. Be on your best behaviour with Uncle Emilio, he's such a good man, he'll give you goat's milk, bread and crackling, honey from his own hives. And make sure you're sensible and polite in Uncle Emilio's house, he's so good, such a fine man. Remember, no catching birds and sticking needles in their eyes, God will punish you if you do, you'll go blind for ever. Learn from Uncle Emilio: he's such a good man because he never killed any birds or poked them in the eye. So you see, you have to be good boys and help pick watercress and wild peppermint for Uncle Emilio, and don't forget to ask for his blessing. Can't we take the ball? No, you're not to, Aunt Lila says, you'll only play and shout too much, you know it upsets Uncle Emilio and scares off his bees.

God bless you, children, says Uncle Emilio, patting our heads. Would you like to come and see my hives, my goats, my melons, my chaffinches, my beds of flowers? No, thanks very much, Uncle, we want to go down to the pitch for a while, if you don't mind. Off you go then, boys, but don't play with those slum kids, and don't tease or fight each other. Of course we won't, Uncle Emilio, because God is everywhere and sees all that we do, and one day he's going to come from on high to pass judgement on the living and the dead.

The moment we got to the pitch, we waved to all the kids in the shacks nearby, and they came swarming like flies. *Che*, if you've got a ball we could have a game. Fat chance. But they nodded slyly at the ground: we saw it was littered with toads that had come up out of the stream to catch insects and were hopping all over the pitch.

What's great is that the ball helps you. It bounces all by itself. Sometimes it's a perfect height for a volley. What's not so great is when you have to change toads. You'll be dribbling forward when you're pulled up short with a *Che*! that ball's no good any more, can't you see the poor thing's had it? This one's the ball now. So there's a lot of arguing, shouting. For goodness sake, boys, what are you up to out there? Aunt Lila's voice drifts over.

Carozo and Titilo have chosen two teams. I'm in goal on Carozo's side, Beto is in the other one. There's four slum kids on each side. Plus hundreds of toads, who take turn at being players too: when they're not the ball, they are leaping all over the pitch as though they're joining in. As one lands, another springs into the air; a seething mass of them cavorting up from the stream towards Uncle Emilio's house, heading straight for his flowerbeds.

Titilo suddenly sends through a high ball. Just as one of the kids is about to head it, he remembers what kind of ball it is, so instead he traps it on his chest, and before it reaches the ground – he's a fantastic player – he checks it on one knee, bounces it off his left foot, then shoots with his right as hard as he can. I'm well positioned, and block the shot easily, but I immediately throw it up over the bar: the ball was freezing! Corner! they all shout. I'm trudging back to fetch it when Titilo says leave it, can't you see it's had it. From the corner the next toad sails over, legs spread wide, its belly gleaming white as it spins across the goal mouth, a dangerous ball. I came out too soon, but Carozo saves us with a tremendous volley that's so fierce it catches the other goalie completely unawares, he doesn't even see the ball as it flies past him into the corner of his goal and splatters somewhere in the distance. One–nil to us: Carozo, the kids and I all hug each other.

Don't get dirty boys, will you? Aunt Lila calls from under the magnolia tree. You'll have to come in soon, we're all going to say a prayer together for poor Uncle Jacinto who died.

We don't want to pray or to hear Uncle Jacinto's story yet again. We'd forgotten all about him. We know he had a moustache and wore a wide-brimmed hat because that's how he is in the picture on the wall.

Three times the whirlpool dragged him under and threw him out, Aunt Lila always tells us, as if we didn't already know, and she holds up three white fingers, but nobody could reach him with a branch or a piece of wood, and after the third time he never surfaced again.

It was his own fault he drowned, Titilo and I always reckoned. We often swam in the whirlpools, they were much more fun than still water. You let them carry you down a few feet, then right at the bottom of the whirlpool there's a spot where there's no pull at all, it peters out completely. All you have to do is push up from the bottom out to the side, so you get free from the eddies. You shoot straight back to the surface, you take a deep breath, then down again. It's like a sledge ride, but more exciting. Everybody knows there's no whirlpool on the riverbed – everybody but Uncle Jacinto, of course. The people watching tried to tell him: push out to the side when you're at the bottom, Señor Jacinto, remember the whirlpool will only bring you to the surface three times. They shouted this to him, waving their arms too, in case he was deaf, but there was no reaction. Instead of taking their advice, all he did was wave his arms back, but none of them could understand what he meant. On the bank, they were shouting: Three! and holding up three fingers for him to get the message, and each time he reappeared he held up his fingers: three, seven, then nine of them. Three times, they were shouting, but nothing doing: it was as if he was making his will: three cows, seven goats, nine chaffinches, I leave them all to my beloved brother Emilio. Water was pouring from his moustache and his hat. The whirlpool only gives you three chances. No reaction from Uncle Jacinto. So of course, after the third time, the whirlpool kept him for ever. You can't get much stupider than that, Titilo and I agreed.

What are you standing there like a dummy for? Carozo screams at me as I let the goal in, when I don't see the toad streaking through my legs because I'm daydreaming about Uncle Jacinto. Thank God, the goal is disallowed, because though one bit of the ball did go inside the post, the rest skimmed past. This is the ball now, one of the kids shouts, sprinting off with it. Just as he makes to shoot Titilo blocks him; we scrape it off, and look for another toad.

Titilo is going all out for the equalizer. He knows I'm not so good in the air, so he hits one hard and high, it's going well over the bar, but I jump as high as I can because I can see the toad is headed right for Uncle Emilio's. I manage to get my fingertips to it, but no use, on it flies, spinning round belly up like a whirlpool until it smashes against Uncle Emilio's birdcages. Immediately we hear Aunt Lila's gentle, unsuspecting voice, for the love of God, little ones, leave that toad alone and come in to say your prayers. She's talking about one toad, but we've already got through about twenty.

Foul! Penalty! they all shout. That equalizing penalty is still vivid in my mind. First they were all squabbling about who should take it. It was a big, fat toad, which wouldn't stay still on the penalty spot while they were arguing. Each time they placed it on the little mound of earth, it would hop off back in the direction of the stream. In the end as usual it was Titilo who took the kick. The ball was shoved back on the spot. Titilo stared at it, came sprinting in, then hit a waist-high shot that whistled straight past me. Then we heard Aunt Lila scream as though she were departing this world, toppling into a whirlpool, and saw her dress suddenly change colour as we heard her strangely muted cry, as though she were merely rehearsing it, almost apologetically, as though instead of screaming she was still politely asking, Boys, what have you done, don't forget that God and Uncle Jacinto are watching you from heaven.

Goal! What a goal! Titilo and his team were shouting, hugging Beto. I'm writhing on the ground, spitting out grass I'm so annoyed at myself for letting a goal in and staining Aunt Lila's dress like that. Now she'll think we don't love her. That dress of hers, so white, so embroidered, with all that lace: the toad had burst right in between the two butterflies, all over the smocked bodice of her robe, her peacock and rosette.

There's nothing worse than trying to pray when the sweat is pouring off you. It's impossible to concentrate on Uncle Jacinto's candle-lit portrait. As we pray, we keep sneaking looks at Aunt Lila, who is now sobbing in her petticoat while she washes her dress in a tub. Titilo is staring at the dead man's portrait, but his eyes are gleaming with triumph. I'm still trying to choke back my rage. If only I'd dived a bit further, I could have caught at least one leg of the ball, and pushed it round for a corner. If I'd done that, we'd have won one–nil.

Uncle Emilio, who is praying beside us as if he were counting melons or goats. Aunt Lila, who by the next summer we had forgotten, along with Uncle Jacinto, because we never returned to the hills. Aunt Lila, who believed in so many good things. Aunt Lila, who I heard never managed completely to get rid of the bloodstains on her white dress. Aunt Lila, unaware that we would keep on squashing toads.

Translated by Nick Caistor

Up Among the Eagles

LUISA VALENZUELA

You'll find what I tell you hard to believe, for who knows anything, nowadays, about life in the country? And life here on the mountains, up among the eagles. You get used to it. Oh yes, I can tell you. I who never knew anything but the city, just look at me now, the colour of clay, carrying my buckets of water from the public fountain. Water for myself and water for others. I've been doing it to eke out a living ever since the day I made the foolish mistake of climbing the path that borders the cliff. I climbed up and, looking down at the green dot of the valley below, I decided to stay here for ever. It wasn't that I was afraid, I was just being prudent, as they say: threatening cliffs, beyond imagination – impossible even to consider returning. Everything I owned I traded for food: my shoes, my wristwatch, my key-ring with all the keys (I wouldn't be needing them any more), a ballpoint pen that was almost out of ink.

The only thing of any value I kept is my Polaroid camera, no one wanted it. Up here they don't believe in preserving images, just the opposite: every day they strive to create new images for the moment only. Often they get together to tell each other about the improbable images they've been envisioning. They sit in a circle in the dark on the dirt floor of their communal hut and concentrate on making the vision appear. One day, out of nothing, they materialized a tapestry of non-existent colours and ineffable design, but they decided that it was just a pale reflection of their mental image, and so they broke the circle to return the tapestry to the nothingness from which it had come.

They are strange creatures; normally they speak a language whose meaning they themselves have forgotten. They communicate by interpreting pauses, intonations, facial expressions and sighs. I tried to learn this language of silences, but

17

it seems I haven't got the right accent. At any rate, they speak our language when they refer to trivial matters, the daily needs that have nothing to do with their images. Even so, some words are missing from their vocabulary. For example, they have no word for yesterday or for tomorrow, before or after, or for one of these days. Here everything is now, and always. An unsatisfactory imitation of eternity like the tapestry I have already mentioned. Have mentioned? Oh yes, I'm the only one to use that verb tense: I may also be the only one who has any notion of conjugation. A vice left over from the world down there, knowledge I can't barter because no one wants it.

Will you trade me some beans for a notion of time, I went around asking the women in the market-place, but they shook their heads emphatically. (A notion of time? They looked at me with mistrust. A way of moving on a different plane? That has nothing to do with the knowledge they are after.)

Who dares speak of the passage of time to the inhabitants of this high place where everything endures? Even their bodies endure. Death neither decays nor obliterates them, it merely stops them in their path. Then the others, with exquisite delicacy – a delicacy I've only seen them employ in connection with newly dropped kids or with certain mushrooms – carry the corpse beyond the rushing stream and with precise symmetry arrange it in the exact place it occupied in life. With infinite patience they have succeeded in creating, on the other side, a second town that obliterates time, an unmoving reflection of themselves that gives them a feeling of security because it is mummified, unmodifiable.

They only allow themselves changes in respect of the images. They grow, yes, they grow up and reach adulthood with only a suspicion of old age, remaining more or less the same until they die. In contrast, I discover with horror that I have a sprinkling of grey hairs, and wrinkles are lining my face; premature, of course, but who could keep her youth in this dry air, beneath such intense skies? What will become of me when they discover that time passes in my life, and is leaving its marks?

They are absorbed in other concerns, in trying to retain

visions of what appear to be jewelled palaces and splendours unknown on this earth. They roam around latitudes of awe while all I can do – and very infrequently and with extreme stealth at that – is take a photo of myself. I am down to earth despite living in this elevated land floating among clouds. And they say the altitude deranges those of us who come from sea level. But it is my belief, my fear, that they are the ones who are deranged; it's something ancestral, inexplicable, especially when they are squatting on their haunches, as they almost always are, looking inward in contemplation. I'm always looking outward, I search every road, almost nonchalantly nourishing my fear. They watch me go by carrying water, the pole across my shoulders and the two buckets dangling from it, and I would like to think they do not suspect my fear. This fear has two faces, not at all like the one that kept me from returning after I had climbed the mountain. No, this is not a simple fear; it reflects others, and becomes voracious.

On the other hand, I am here, now. That now grows and changes and expands with time and, if I am lucky, will continue to evolve. I do not want them to be aware of this evolving, as I have already said, and even less do I want to be like them, exempt from time. For what would become of me if I kept this face for ever, as if surprised between two ages? I think about the mummies in the mirror city, oh yes, absolutely, only mummies are unchanged by time. Time does not pass for the dead, I told myself one day, and on a different day (because I, if not they, am very careful to relate question to calendar) I added: nor does it pass for those who have no concept of death. Death is a milestone.

The inhabitants here, with their language of silence, could teach me the secrets of the immobility that so closely resembles immortality, but I am not eager to learn them. Life is a movement towards death; to remain static is to be already dead.

Sit here, little lady, nice and quiet here with us is one of the few things they consent to say to me in my own language, and I shake my head energetically (one more way of ensuring movement), and as soon as I am out of their sight, I begin to run like crazy along the neglected paths. More often than not

I run up, not down, but either way, I don't want to get too far from the town, I don't want to stumble into the still city and find myself face-to-face with the mummies.

The secret city. I don't know its exact location but I know everything about it – or maybe I only suspect. I know it has to be identical to this humble little clump of huts where we live, a faithful replica with exactly the same number of bodies, for when one of them dies the oldest mummy is thrown into the void. It's noisy in the secret city. The noise announces its proximity, but it also serves a more basic purpose; scraps of tin, of every size and shape, hang from the rafters of the huts to scare away the buzzards. They are all that moves in the secret city, those scraps of tin to scare away the vultures, the only thing that moves or makes a sound. On certain limpid nights the wind carries the sound to where the living dwell, and on those nights they gather in the plaza, and dance.

They dance, but oh so slowly, almost without moving their feet, more as if they were undulating, submerged in the dense waters of sound. This happens only rarely, and when it does I feel an almost uncontrollable urge to join in the dance – the need to dance soaks into my bones, sways me – but I resist with all my strength. I am afraid that nothing could be more paralysing than to yield to this music that comes from death. So that I won't be paralysed I don't dance. I don't dance and I don't share the visions.

I have not witnessed a birth since I have been here. I know they couple, but they don't reproduce. They do nothing to avoid it, simply the stillness of the air prevents it. As for me, at this point I don't go near men. It must be admitted that men don't come near me either, and there must be a reason, considering how often and how closely they approach almost anything else. Something in my expression must drive them away, but I've no way of knowing what it is. There are no mirrors here. No reflections. Water is either glaucous or torrential white. I despair. And very often in the privacy of my cave, sparingly and with extreme caution, I take a new photo of myself.

I do this when I can't stand things any longer, when I have an overwhelming need to know about myself, and then no fear, no caution, can hold me back. One problem is that I am running out of film. In addition, I know perfectly well that if they find my photographs, if they place them in chronological order, two things can happen: they will either abominate or adore me. And neither possibility is to be desired. There are no alternatives. If they put the photos in order and draw the conclusions. If they see that when I arrived, my face was smoother, my hair brighter, my bearing more alert. If they discover the marks of time they will know that I have not controlled time even for a moment. And so if they find I am growing older, they won't want me among them, and they will stone me out of town, and I will have to face the terrifying cliffs.

I don't even want to think about the other possibility. That they will adore me because I have so efficiently, and so concretely, materialized these images of myself. Then I would be like stone to them, like a statue forever captive and contained.

Either of these two lapidary prospects should provide sufficient reason to restrain my suicidal impulse to take yet another photograph, but it doesn't. Each time, I succumb, hoping against hope that they will not be alerted by the glare of the flash. Sometimes I choose stormy nights; perhaps I conjure up the lightning with my pale simulacrum. At other times I seek the protective radiance of dawn, which at this altitude can be incendiary.

Elaborate preparations for each of my secret snapshots, preparations charged with hope and danger. That is, with life. The resulting picture does not always please me but the emotion of seeing myself – no matter how horrible or haggard I appear – is immeasurable. This is I, changing in a static world that imitates death. And I feel safe. Then I am able to stop and speak of simple things with the women in the market and even understand their silences, and answer them. I can live a little longer without love, without anyone's touch.

Until another relapse, a new photo. And this will be the last. On a day with the sound of death, when the minimal activities of the town have come to a halt and they have all congregated to dance in the market-place. That deliberate dancing that is like praying with their feet, a quiet prayer.

They will never admit it, but I suspect that they count to themselves, that their dance is an intricate web of steps like knitting, one up, two backwards, one to the right. All to the tinkling of the far-off tin scraps: the wind in the house of the dead. A day like any other; a very special day for them because of the sound that they would call music, were they interested in making such distinctions. But all that interests them is the dance, or believing they are dancing, or thinking of the dance, which is the same thing. To the pulse of the sound that floods over us, whose origins I cannot locate though I know it comes from the city of the dead.

They do not call to me, they don't even see me. It's as if I didn't exist. Maybe they're right, maybe I don't exist, maybe I am my own invention, or a peculiar materialization of an image they have evoked. That sound is joyful, and yet the most mournful ever heard. I seem to be alive, and yet . . .

I hide in my cave trying not to think, trying not to hear the tinkling; I don't know where it comes from, but I fear where it may lead me. With the hope of setting these fears to rest, I begin my preparations for the last photo: a desperate attempt to recover my being. To return to myself, which is all I have.

Anxiously, I wait for the perfect moment, while outside, darkness is weaving its blackest threads. Suddenly, an unexpected radiance causes me to trip the shutter before I am ready. No photograph emerges, only a dark rectangle that gradually reveals the blurred image of a stone wall. And that's all. I have no more film so I may as well throw away the camera. A cause for weeping were it not for the fact the radiance is not fading. A cause for uneasiness, then, because when I peer out I see that the blazing light is originating from the very place I wanted not to know about, from the very heart of the sound, from a peak just below us. And the radiance comes from millions of glittering scraps of tin in the moonlight. The city of the dead.

Spontaneously, I set forth with all my stupid photos, responding to an impulse that responds, perhaps, to a summons from the sonorous radiance. They are calling me from down there, over to the left, and I answer, and at first I run along the treacherous path and when the path ends I continue on. I stumble, I climb and descend, I trip and hurt myself; to avoid hurtling into the ravine I try to imitate the goats, leaping across the rocks; I lose my footing, I slip and slide, I try to check my fall, thorns rake my skin and at the same time hold me back. Rashly I pull ahead and it is imperative that I reach the city of the dead and leave my face to the mummies. I will place my successive faces on the mummies and then at last I'll be free to go down without fearing stone for I'll take my last photo with me and I am myself in that photo and I am stone.

Translated by Margaret Sayers Peden

BRAZIL

Alaindelon de la Patrie

JOÃO UBALDO RIBEIRO

I do not understand him who has a liking for bulls and cows. There was a time here when they used to raise a great many humpbacked Indian cattle, which to me have faces signifying deceit, lies, crimes and shamelessness. In addition, most of them have dark circles around their eyes, which shows them to be evil-minded perverts not to be trusted. Any man who has found himself in the pasture or even in the corral in the company of a humpback knows he cannot turn his back or allow himself to be off-guard, because the humpback may get him, and if he does will not treat him sympathetically. As far as I am concerned, being otherwise employed at this farm mostly for general duties, the only bull that gets along fine with me is the one known as Big Butt, who is already a bit stricken in years and a very gentlemanly Dutch bull. In Big Butt's case, when the need arises I go and take care of him, and if I am not joy itself when I do it, at least I do it in peace and quiet, since the Dutch bull is by nature a civil and well-versed creature, and one can readily see his Dutchness. This must be because in his homeland they have kings and queens and ever since bulls have been bulls in Dutchland they have been brought up to observe the proprieties. So the Dutch bull covers his cows with a great feeling for his obligations, and it is a beautiful thing to watch, because Dutch cows are also most well mannered, and so when Big Butt is doing his job with one of them even our visitors enjoy watching, because he dismounts the cow with much elegance and almost a thank you and a smile from her. It is a most polished thing. This bull Big Butt, by the way, enjoys a few peanuts in the *bagasse* whenever I can oblige him, since he is getting old and needs to be able to unfurl his instrument in order to maintain steady employment – for when Big Butt is no longer a swordsman, goodbye Big Butt, and maybe I shall even miss

27

him for although he is not really anybody's close friend, the way he treats me you would think he has at least a secondary school diploma. If some day I eat a stew made of some part of Big Butt, I shall eat it with sorrow. I shall eat it because life is one eating the other, and it is better for us to eat the bull than the bull to eat us; it is a political matter, even more so because the bull does not speak.

In the old days it used not to be like this, I mean, we did not have all this organization. The humpback formerly in charge of servicing the cows was quite outrageous. Called Nonô of Bombay, this humpbacked bull would keep hoofing up the dust among the cows of his race, and when one of them forgot to keep an eye on him, you would think he was a paying customer entitled to the whole works and the cow would not even have time to get into the proper position because Nonô would rush at her snorting smoke and ready for action, and one thing I thank God for is that He did not bring me into this world to be one of that humpback's cows. In fact, there were more than a few times when the cowhands had to adjust him for a proper entrance because he did not pay attention to how things were done, he would dab any part of a cow wherever he found one. A very backward type, the king of uncouth. When I remember Nonô of Bombay having intercourse with his cows I shiver, for the cow suffered much. When a man compares the way Big Butt treated his Dutch cows to the way Nonô treated his humpbacks, he sees the difference between a blond, cultured person such as Big Butt and an unprincipled, mulatto person such as Nonô. This is one of the many reasons why in my next reincarnation, God willing, I will come back white and well educated. I do not wish to act like Nonô, who almost tore his cows apart, even though he is quite well admired around these parts and the story goes that to this day there are women who, enthusiastically playing the two-backed beast, praise their men by saying, 'Let me have it, my Nonô!' but I consider those women to be a bunch of humpbacked cows, that is what I think, because I am in favour of tenderness, and blows should only be used when pleaded for or truly deserved.

However, with all the Nonôs and Big Butts and a few more

stud-bulls of some repute in this land, such carryings on have always been pretty standard. The rooster sometimes seems to be conversing with his shadow or discussing elections or something when all of a sudden he flares up with great brilliance and begins pecking the chickens back and forth and puffing himself up in the direction of their tails, and thus he does all his work in something like five minutes, spark-like. The eggs that follow are brown, not white, fertile, not barren, and quite good for one's health, or else out come little chicks and all the chickens go on with their chickening as Our Lord wished. Thus the little lizard has two rods, one at the right, one at the left, so that any female lizard can be well provided whether she be left or right, and it should be said that the lizard only catches one lizardess at a time, not taking advantage of being able to serve two. For it is not a matter of vanity, it is a question of not wasting time, because if it is true that the lizard has many flies to eat, it is also true that there are many other creatures who want to eat the lizard, so he cannot afford to take it easy. The hummingbird makes it in the air, sometimes just in passing, sometimes giving a greeting and profiting by the opportunity, since the hummingbird's heart beats so fast it buzzes, and he dies an early death, his heart buzzing, his flowers being kissed. Jenny donkeys and mares much appreciate being mounted by the male, and there are cases of she-donkeys that keep on giving a jackass little kicks all afternoon until they get him, and then they grind their teeth and drool a little and become great admirers of the male, if it turns out he knew how to answer those little kicks well. The land tortoise grunts when he is on top of the female, and she shows great patience because their construction does not make things easy, and that must be why he grunts. The pig and the drake apply screws, and there are those who say the screws are to stupefy the female, for she stares and stares until the screws get the better of her. The cat produces thorns which make the she-cat bleed as he withdraws, the bleeding, however, being necessary for her to become pregnant. The praying mantis stands motionless, and even before she is finished she begins to chew him up and there is room for all of him inside her belly. All of this can be seen here and many more things, from the lagoons with their toads and frogs getting married all across the waters to the noises of the biggest creatures. This is the way Nature was made and in each and every coupling you can feel her strength.

Well then, in these modern times we have been unnaturalized. Although I, disliking all kinds of bulls, did not know very well what was happening until everything started changing and we began being visited by many doctors and important persons. And it so happened that after many pronouncements and great nervousness, we took the large cage to the railway station, like a party lacking only a musical band, to greet the great French Charolais bull who even before arriving here had been given the name Alaindelon. All French names end in *on*, and the name was supposed to be Napoleon, another tremendous Frenchman, who invaded England, chased King John the Sixth out of Portugal and all in all raised a great perturbation everywhere and wouldn't let anyone get away with anything. But Alaindelon was the final choice, being the name of a French movie star of very great reputation and from what I hear about this Alaindelon one would expect the cows here to be celebrating vastly.

Now, it seemed to me as soon as I saw him that this here Alaindelon was a wholly sorrowful animal, wrapped in darkness and apparently in mourning. At first I thought it was just the nature of French bulls, because it's well known that Frenchmen have a strong penchant for lechering but always with the utmost decency, not like Nonô of Bombay. But even so how could this bull be so sad, since it was also well known that from now on he would be installed like a monarch, with massages, special food, stroking and vitamins? And if the cows he was supposed to work with were not French cows of the highest upbringing, they were not something you would throw out of the window either, and it should be added that it was the beginning of summer and a general carnality was taking over in all parts of the farm, even the blowflies giving the lady blowflies their best, the boy earwigs with the girl earwigs and so forth, not to mention others, such as the cavies, which as everybody knows are always either eating or employing their lovemaking tools, be it summer or winter. And sometimes a man dresses in black like this but it does not mean a thing, witness for instance Father Barretinho, God keep his soul, may more words on this never escape my lips.

A job such as this many of us spend our lives praying to find, and now he arrives with all this sadness and showing himself to be almost disagreeable. An animal as big as a stocky elephant, all in black and with a disheartened countenance one could not help feeling sorry for, when the natural thing for him would be to be swishing his tail, drooling a little and preparing his gear. But this is evidence that the animal also has intelligence, because our Alaindelon already had a perfect knowledge of what was going to happen, which was why he was not rejoicing and, poor fellow, he had reason completely on his side.

When I found out, it staggered me. For about a week or two Alaindelon had been installed in his apartment with ventilation and all perquisites, including an American apparatus to stop the flies from bothering him, and then, as I passed by to fetch a few buckets and some troughs, I asked when his holiday would be over and he would go out to work on some cows.

'Given his great fame, everybody here wishes to get a look,' I said. 'He must be a thing of great competence.'

'But he won't be working on any cows,' answered Dr Crescêncio, who works here as a kind of cow engineer, giving directions, and has a college degree in cows.

'So, what is he here for? Isn't he a stud?'

'Do you think we would waste an animal like him directly with the cows? No sir! Everything that comes from him is worth gold. What we do is to extract the material, put it on ice, and stick it in the cows with a needle. That way nothing is wasted.'

At this point I saw Alaindelon's face poking out of an opening, and I realized that he must already know Brazilian, maybe he studied it in France, because he understood the whole conversation and became even more downcast than before, and such a grief it was that it made one's heart bleed. I inquired as to how the material was to be extracted, whether it meant that they would stick a needle in the poor animal's masculine pouch, but Dr Crescêncio said no. Every so many days, he said, the people in charge will come to do the manipulation.

'How does this manipulation work?'

'You can watch if you wish for we are going to collect a few minutes from now.'

'And does it not upset the bull, Doctor?'

'Not at all, he is accustomed to it.'

And, indeed, Alaindelon, if he was not enthusiastic, did not raise any difficulties either, one could see he was practised in his profession. As soon as he caught sight of the manipulation team, he spread his legs apart and looked the other way and then let himself be extracted, everything very businesslike, without so much as a little sigh. By then one could not help feeling very, very sorry to see a prestigious, medal-covered animal subject to being called a virgin stud. At the very end the manipulators even gave him a little squeeze, but he never protested, he stood there putting up with such humiliations in the best possible mood. How can a mortal endure such a situation – especially a Frenchman?

Maybe his profession is more respected in France than it is here, because here things are the way they are, so he received several nicknames – Five-against-one, Cold Hose, Knows-no-Cow, Windfucker, Drip-in-the-jug, Hand Sausage, a whole lot of them – and we laughed but we also felt that it was not right to make fun of somebody's misfortune like that.

That was why we decided on a plan to do Alaindelon a benefaction, this benefaction to be carried out by the cow Honey Blossom, short on breeding but with a strong rump and a good build, and also a cow of much experience in life, having even been, according to some, Nonô of Bombay's mistress, and people say that the two of them used to eat a couple of hemp plants, also known as Angolan tobacco, better yet marijuana – what are we trying to hide – which grows here like so much bristlegrass, and not a few take a little smoke now and then, well, people say that the two of them would eat a couple of saplings and get into a great deal of indecency. This was before Nonô caught foot-and-mouth disease during a binge and died old and sore in the mouth and disapproved of by everyone in general. One acknowledges therefore that Honey Blossom was no young maiden, but in the first place it is known that Frenchmen appreciate older women. And second, Honey Blossom was always in the mood, which is something you cannot say about all cows, even if they are cows or maybe actually because of that.

So Emanuel and I and also the boy Ruidenor agreed to take Honey Blossom to the small corral which is close to Alaindelon's apartment, and during the night we would go there and release the Frenchman. No sooner said than done, and we even had moonlight to make things perfect. We startled him when we opened the door, he was not used to that. And there was no way to make him come out, even with us doing a lot of explaining. Emanuel went as far as to suggest we flick his thingamabob to see if that got him in the mood, but we all feared he might presume one of us to be a manipulator and then wish to have the job finished, and a bull of this size one should try not to displease. But we tried so hard that he finally inched out into the corral, just a little suspicious. At that point Honey Blossom, proving herself to be quite a hot-blooded old girl, flared her nostrils towards Alaindelon and came closer and closer, but he did not even seem to notice.

'Do you think they manipulated him just a short time ago and he is now weakened?' Emanuel asked.

'No way, no way!' said Ruidenor, who was dying to see the whole business take place. 'Pull him closer to her, pull him closer.'

I do not know how many tons a dunderhead like that bull weighs, but we went on pulling and tugging and 'go Alaindelon, go Alaindelon!' and Honey Blossom standing by more than willing, and the only thing we did not do was to put a heavy duty jack under the unfortunate bull to make him rise, all to no avail. And then, when everybody was already about to give up, he looked one way and then the other, looked at me and then at Emanuel, and made a weak little motion upwards to climb on the cow's back, and quick as a wink she put herself in the right position, because the old she-devil still wanted very much to enjoy the Frenchman.

'There he goes, there he goes! Have faith, Alaindelon!'

But it seems that French bulls are bulls of little faith, because halfway through that weak little rise that everybody doubted would ever reach Honey Blossom's height, Alaindelon rolled his eyeballs, made a little noise in his throat and spilled his stuff all over the earth.

'Holy Mother, there must be more than seven hundred thousand in good money sprinkling the dust right there!' Emanuel said. 'Let's take that bull back inside!'

And truly, in a situation like this, the only possible thing to do was to take him back looking very ashamed and Honey Blossom most annoyed and as far as we know feeling quite nostalgic about Nonô of Bombay. The next day, not a word from us because of how Alaindelon's raw material had been wasted. But apparently no one noticed because, although we were nervous when the time came for the next manipulation, Alaindelon worked just the same as usual and nobody complained about his output. Only we three noticed that whenever he saw us he became quite discomfited, but we understood and respected it, so no one made any comments. And anyway it was revealed that Alaindelon was a kind of corporation, because no one had enough money to buy him all for himself, so he spent some time producing on a certain farm and then another and another and so on. And the day came for us to put him back in the same cage and take him back to the train once again. It cannot be said that he made friends here, but neither did he make any enemies. And all three of us knew for sure that he was born to his profession, and that was the only way he knew how to work – he was a specialist – there was nothing anyone could do. Just the same, Emanuel stroked his head at boarding time and said, 'May God help you find a good hand, Alaindelon.' And the owner of the farm overheard, but did not ask about it, happy as he was with the money he'd made from the Frenchman's work. When the train rolled on, he sang in a soft voice:

'Alaindelon de la Patri-i-i-i-e!'

He thinks I didn't understand, but I did. He sang a piece of the French anthem, only substituting Alaindelon for Napoleon. In French, it means 'Alaindelon of our motherland.' Theirs, not mine.

Translated by the author

Peace and War

MOACYR SCLIAR

I was late for the war; I had to take a taxi. A setback: with the recent fare increase, it was an unforeseen and unwelcome expense, a blow to my budget. Nevertheless, I arrived just in time to clock on, thereby avoiding greater problems. There was a long queue next to the clocking-on machine: I wasn't the only laggard. There was Walter, my trench colleague, grumbling: he'd had to take a taxi too. We were neighbours and we had entered the war almost at the same time. On the second Thursday of every month we caught the bus from the corner of the street, to take part in the hostilities.

'I'm fed up with this business,' said Walter.

'So am I,' I replied.

Sighing, we punched our cards and headed for the administration shed where the cloakroom had temporarily (more than fifteen years ago) been installed.

'Late today?' asked the youth in charge of the cloakroom.

We didn't bother to reply. We took the keys to our lockers. We quickly changed our clothes, putting on our old campaign uniforms, collected our rifles and ammunition (twenty cartridges) and made our way to the front line.

The setting for the conflict was open country, on the outskirts of the city. The battlefield was fenced off with barbed wire posted with signboards: WAR, KEEP OUT. An unnecessary warning: few people came there to that place of cottages and summer retreats.

We, the soldiers, occupied a trench almost two kilometres long. An enemy, whom we never saw, was about one kilometre away, also entrenched. The ground between the two trenches was strewn with debris: wrecked armoured cars and tanks mingled with the bones of horses, a reminder of a time when the struggle had been fierce. Now the conflict had entered a stable phase – a holding operation, in the words of our commander. Battles no longer occurred. The only piece of advice they gave us was not to get out of the trench. A problem for me: my younger son wanted an empty shell cartridge, which I had not been able to obtain. The boy kept asking for it; I could do nothing.

We went down into the trench, Walter and I. The place was not altogether uncomfortable. We had tables, chairs, a small stove, cooking utensils, not to mention a record-player and a portable TV. I suggested a game of cards.

'Later,' he said. He was examining his rifle with a furrowed brow and an air of annoyance.

'This lousy thing doesn't work any more,' he announced.

'Well,' I said, 'it's over fifteen years old, it's already given all it had to give.' And I offered him my weapon. At that moment we heard a crack and the whine of a bullet over our heads.

'That was close,' I said.

'Those idiots,' grumbled Walter. 'One of these days they'll end up hurting someone.' He took my weapon, stood up and fired two shots into the air.

'Let that be a warning to you,' he shouted, and sat down again. An orderly appeared, with a cordless telephone: 'Your wife, Mr Walter.'

'The Devil take her!' he exclaimed. 'Even here she won't leave me in peace.' He picked up the phone.

'Hello! Yes, it's me. I'm fine. Of course I'm fine. No, nothing's happened to me, I've already told you I'm fine. I know you get nervous, but there's no need. Everything's all right. I'm well wrapped up, it's not raining. Did you hear? Everything's fine. No need to apologize. I understand. Bye bye.'

'What a pain that woman is,' he said, handing the telephone back to the orderly. I said nothing. I too had a problem with my wife, but a different one: she didn't believe that we were at war. She suspected I spent the day in a motel. I would have liked to explain to her what sort of war this was, but to tell the truth I didn't know. No one did. It was a very confusing thing; so much so that a commission had been set up to study the situation. The chairman of the commission came to visit us from time to time, and complained about the car he'd been given for his tours of inspection: an old banger, according to him. For reasons of economy they refused to change it.

All was quiet on the front that morning; one of us fired a shot, those on the other side replied, and that was it. At midday they served lunch. Green salad, roast meat and Greek rice, followed by a tasteless pudding.

'This is getting worse and worse,' complained Walter. The orderly asked him if he thought he was in a restaurant, or what. Walter didn't reply.

We lay down for our afternoon nap and slept peacefully. When we awoke, night was falling.

'I think I'll be off now,' I said to Walter. He couldn't come with me: he was on duty that night. I went to the cloakroom, changed my clothes.

'How was the war?' the cheeky youth asked.

'Fine,' I replied, 'just fine.' I called into admin to collect my cheque from a sour-faced official. I signed the three copies of the receipt. I got to the bus-stop in plenty of time.

At home, my wife was waiting for me in her leotard. I'm ready, she said, drily. I went to the bedroom and put on my kit. We went into the study, climbed on to our ergometric bicycles.

'Where were we, then?' I asked.

'You never seem to know,' she replied. She picked up the map, studied it for a moment and said: 'Bisceglie, on the Adriatic coast.'

We began to pedal furiously. Two hours later, when we stopped, we were near Molfetta, still on the Adriatic. We're hoping to do Italy in a year. After that, we'll see. I don't like to make long-term plans; because of the war, naturally, but even more because keeping the future unknown is a source of permanent excitement.

Translated by Tricia Feeney

CHILE

The Judge's Wife

ISABEL ALLENDE

Nicolas Vidal always knew he would lose his head over a woman. So it was foretold on the day of his birth, and later confirmed by the Turkish woman in the corner shop the one time he allowed her to read his fortune in the coffee grounds. Little did he imagine though that it would be on account of Casilda, Judge Hidalgo's wife. It was on her wedding day that he first glimpsed her. He was not impressed, preferring his women dark-haired and brazen. This ethereal slip of a girl in her wedding gown, eyes filled with wonder, and fingers obviously unskilled in the art of rousing a man to pleasure, seemed to him almost ugly. Mindful of his destiny, he had always been wary of any emotional contact with women, hardening his heart and restricting himself to the briefest of encounters whenever the demands of manhood needed satisfying. Casilda, however, appeared so insubstantial, so distant, that he cast aside all precaution and, when the fateful moment arrived, forgot the prediction that usually weighed in all his decisions. From the roof of the bank, where he was crouching with two of his men, Nicolas Vidal peered down at this young lady from the capital. She had a dozen equally pale and dainty relatives with her, who spent the whole of the ceremony fanning themselves with an air of utter bewilderment, then departed straight away, never to return. Along with everyone else in the town, Vidal was convinced the young bride would not withstand the climate, and that within a few months the old women would be dressing her up again, this time for her funeral. Even if she did survive the heat and the dust that filtered in through every pore to lodge itself in the soul, she would be bound to succumb to the fussy habits of her confirmed bachelor of a husband. Judge Hidalgo was twice her age, and had slept alone for so many years he didn't have the slightest notion of how to go about pleasing a

41

woman. The severity and stubbornness with which he executed the law even at the expense of justice had made him feared throughout the province. He refused to apply any common sense in the exercise of his profession, and was equally harsh in his condemnation of the theft of a chicken as of a premeditated murder. He dressed formally in black, and, despite the all-pervading dust in this god-forsaken town, his boots always shone with beeswax. A man such as he was never meant to be a husband, and yet not only did the gloomy wedding-day prophecies remain unfulfilled, but Casilda emerged happy and smiling from three pregnancies in rapid succession. Every Sunday at noon she would go to mass with her husband, cool and collected beneath her Spanish mantilla, seemingly untouched by our pitiless summer, as wan and frail-looking as on the day of her arrival: a perfect example of delicacy and refinement. Her loudest words were a soft-spoken greeting; her most expressive gesture was a graceful nod of the head. She was such an airy, diaphanous creature that a moment's carelessness might mean she disappeared altogether. So slight an impression did she make that the changes noticeable in the Judge were all the more remarkable. Though outwardly he remained the same – he still dressed as black as a crow and was as stiff-necked and brusque as ever – his judgments in court altered dramatically. To general amazement, he found the youngster who robbed the Turkish shopkeeper innocent, on the grounds that she had been selling him short for years, and the money he had taken could therefore be seen as compensation. He also refused to punish an adulterous wife, arguing that since her husband himself kept a mistress he did not have the moral authority to demand fidelity. Word in the town had it that the Judge was transformed the minute he crossed the threshold at home: that he flung off his gloomy apparel, rollicked with his children, chuckled as he sat Casilda on his lap. Though no one ever succeeded in confirming these rumours, his wife got the credit for his new-found kindness, and her reputation grew accordingly. None of this was of the slightest interest to Nicolas Vidal, who as a wanted man was sure there would be no mercy shown him the day he was brought in chains before the Judge. He paid no heed to the talk about Doña Casilda, and the rare occasions he glimpsed her from afar only confirmed his first impression of her as a lifeless ghost.

Born thirty years earlier in a windowless room in the town's only brothel, Vidal was the son of Juana the Forlorn and an unknown father. The world had no place for him. His mother knew it, and so tried to wrench him from her womb with sprigs of parsley, candle butts, douches of ashes and other violent purgatives, but the child clung to life. Once, years later, Juana was looking at her mysterious son and realized that, while all her infallible methods of aborting might have failed to dislodge him, they had none the less tempered his soul to the hardness of iron. As soon as he came into the world, he was lifted in the air by the midwife who examined him by the light of an oil-lamp. She saw he had four nipples.

'Poor creature: he'll lose his head over a woman,' she predicted, drawing on her wealth of experience.

Her words rested on the boy like a deformity. Perhaps a woman's love would have made his existence less wretched. To atone for all her attempts to kill him before birth, his mother chose him a beautiful first name, and an imposing family name picked at random. But the lofty name of Nicolas Vidal was no protection against the fateful cast of his destiny. His face was scarred from knife fights before he reached his teens, so it came as no surprise to decent folk that he ended up a bandit. By the age of twenty, he had become the leader of a band of desperadoes. The habit of violence toughened his sinews. The solitude he was condemned to for fear of falling prey to a woman lent his face a doleful expression. As soon as they saw him, everyone in the town knew from his eyes, clouded by tears he would never allow to fall, that he was the son of Juana the Forlorn. Whenever there was an outcry after a crime had been committed in the region, the police set out with dogs to track him down, but after scouring the hills invariably returned empty-handed. In all honesty they preferred it that way, because they could never have fought him. His gang gained such a fearsome reputation that the surrounding villages and estates paid to keep them away. This money would have been plenty for his men, but Nicolas Vidal kept them constantly on horseback in a whirlwind of death and destruction so they would not lose their taste for battle. Nobody dared take them on. More than once, Judge Hidalgo had asked the government to send troops to reinforce the police, but after several useless forays the soldiers returned to their barracks and Nicolas Vidal's gang to their exploits. On one occasion only did Vidal come close to falling into the hands of justice, and then he was saved by his hardened heart.

Weary of seeing the laws flouted, Judge Hidalgo resolved to forget his scruples and set a trap for the outlaw. He realized that to defend justice he was committing an injustice, but chose the lesser of two evils. The only bait he could find was Juana the Forlorn, as she was Vidal's sole known relative. He had her dragged from the brothel where by now, since no clients were willing to pay for her exhausted charms, she scrubbed floors and cleaned out the lavatories. He put her in a specially made cage which was set up in the middle of the Plaza de Armas, with only a jug of water to meet her needs.

'As soon as the water's finished, she'll start to squawk. Then her son will come running, and I'll be waiting for him with the soldiers,' Judge Hidalgo said.

News of this torture, unheard of since the days of slavery, reached Nicolas Vidal's ears shortly before his mother drank the last of the water. His men watched as he received the report in silence, without so much as a flicker of emotion on his blank lone wolf's face, or a pause in the sharpening of his dagger blade on a leather strap. Though for many years he had had no contact with Juana, and retained few happy childhood memories, this was a question of honour. No man can accept such an insult, his gang reasoned as they got guns and horses ready to rush into the ambush and, if need be, lay down their lives. Their chief showed no sign of being in a hurry. As the hours went by tension mounted in the camp. The perspiring, impatient men stared at each other, not daring to speak. Fretful, they caressed the butts of their revolvers and their horses' manes, or busied themselves coiling their lassos. Night fell. Nicolas Vidal was the only one in the camp who slept. At dawn, opinions were divided. Some of the men reckoned he was even more heartless than they had ever imagined, while others maintained their leader was planning a spectacular ruse to free his mother. The one thing that never crossed any of their minds was that his courage might have failed him, for he had always proved he had more than enough to spare. By noon, they could bear the suspense no longer, and went to ask him what he planned to do.

'I'm not going to fall into his trap like an idiot,' he said.

'What about your mother?'

'We'll see who's got more balls, the Judge or me,' Nicolas Vidal coolly replied.

By the third day, Juana the Forlorn's cries for water had ceased. She lay curled on the cage floor, with wildly staring eyes and swollen lips, moaning softly whenever she regained consciousness, and the rest of the time dreaming she was in hell. Four armed guards stood watch to make sure nobody brought her water. Her groans penetrated the entire town, filtering through closed shutters or being carried by the wind through the cracks in doors. They got stuck in corners, where dogs worried at them, and passed them on in their howls to the newly born, so that whoever heard them was driven to distraction. The Judge couldn't prevent a steady stream of people filing through the square to show their sympathy for the old woman, and was powerless to stop the prostitutes going on a sympathy strike just as the miners' fortnight holiday was beginning. That Saturday, the streets were thronged with lusty workmen desperate to unload their savings, who now found nothing in town apart from the spectacle of the cage and this universal wailing carried mouth to mouth down from the river to the coast road. The priest headed a group of Catholic ladies to plead with Judge Hidalgo for Christian mercy and to beg him to spare the poor old innocent woman such a frightful death, but the man of the law bolted his door and refused to listen to them. It was then they decided to turn to Doña Casilda.

The Judge's wife received them in her shady living room. She listened to their pleas looking, as always, bashfully down at the floor. Her husband had not been home for three days, having locked himself in his office to wait for Nicolas Vidal to fall into his trap. Without so much as glancing out of the window, she was aware of what was going on, for Juana's long-drawn-out agony had forced its way even into the vast rooms of her residence. Doña Casilda waited until her visitors had left, dressed her children in their Sunday best, tied a black ribbon round their arms as a token of mourning, then strode out with them in the direction of the square. She carried a food hamper and a bottle of fresh water for Juana the Forlorn. When the guards spotted her turning the corner, they realized what she was up to, but they had strict orders, and barred her way with their rifles. When, watched now by a small crowd, she persisted, they grabbed her by the arms. Her children began to cry.

Judge Hidalgo sat in his office overlooking the square. He was the only person in the town who had not stuffed wax in his ears, because his mind was intent on the ambush and he was straining to catch the sound of horses' hoofs, the signal for action. For three long days and nights he put up with Juana's groans and the insults of the townspeople gathered outside the courtroom, but when he heard his own children start to wail he knew he had reached the bounds of his endurance. Vanquished, he walked out of the office with his three days' beard, his eyes bloodshot from keeping watch, and the weight of a thousand years on his back. He crossed the street, turned into the square and came face to face with his wife. They gazed at each other sadly. In seven years, this was the first time she had gone against him, and she had chosen to do so in front of the whole town. Easing the hamper and the bottle from Casilda's grasp, Judge Hidalgo himself opened the cage to release the prisoner.

'Didn't I tell you he wouldn't have the balls?' laughed Nicolas Vidal when the news reached him.

His laughter turned sour the next day, when he heard that Juana the Forlorn had hanged herself from the chandelier in the brothel where she had spent her life, overwhelmed by the shame of her only son leaving her to fester in a cage in the middle of the Plaza de Armas.

'That Judge's hour has come,' said Vidal.

He planned to take the Judge by surprise, put him to a

horrible death, then dump him in the accursed cage for all to see. The Turkish shopkeeper sent him word that the Hidalgo family had left that same night for a seaside resort to rid themselves of the bitter taste of defeat.

The Judge learned he was being pursued when he stopped to rest at a wayside inn. There was little protection for him there until an army patrol could arrive, but he had a few hours' start, and his motor car could outrun the gang's horses. He calculated he could make it to the next town and summon help there. He ordered his wife and children into the car, put his foot down on the accelerator and sped off along the road. He ought to have arrived with time to spare, but it had been ordained that Nicolas Vidal was that day to meet the woman who would lead him to his doom.

Overburdened by the sleepless nights, the townspeople's hostility, the blow to his pride and the stress of this race to save his family, Judge Hidalgo's heart gave a massive jolt, then split like a pomegranate. The car ran out of control, turned several somersaults and finally came to a halt in the ditch. It took Doña Casilda some minutes to work out what had happened. Her husband's advancing years had often led her to think what it would be like to be left a widow, yet she had never imagined he would leave her at the mercy of his enemies. She wasted little time dwelling on her situation, knowing she must act at once to get her children to safety. When she gazed around her, she almost burst into tears. There was no sign of life in the vast plain baked by a scorching sun, only barren cliffs beneath an unbounded sky bleached colourless by the fierce light. A second look revealed the dark shadow of a passage or cave on a distant slope, so she ran towards it with two children in her arms and the third clutching her skirts.

One by one she carried her children up the cliff. The cave was a natural one, typical of many in the region. She peered inside to be certain it wasn't the den of some wild animal, sat her children against its back wall, then, dry-eyed, kissed them goodbye.

'The troops will come to find you a few hours from now. Until then, don't for any reason whatsoever come out of here, even if you hear me screaming – do you understand?'

Their mother gave one final glance at the terrified children clinging to each other, then clambered back down to the road. She reached the car, closed her husband's eyes, smoothed back her hair and settled down to wait. She had no idea how many men were in Nicolas Vidal's gang, but prayed there were a lot of them so it would take them all the more time to have their way with her. She gathered strength pondering on how long it would take her to die if she determined to do it as slowly as possible. She willed herself to be desirable, luscious, to create more work for them and thus gain time for her children.

Casilda did not have long to wait. She soon saw a cloud of dust on the horizon and heard the gallop of horses' hoofs. She clenched her teeth. Then, to her astonishment, she saw there was only one rider, who stopped a few yards from her, gun at the ready. By the scar on his face she recognized Nicolas Vidal, who had set out all alone in pursuit of Judge Hidalgo, as this was a private matter between the two men. The Judge's wife understood she was going to have to endure something far worse than a lingering death.

A quick glance at her husband was enough to convince Vidal that the Judge was safely out of his reach in the peaceful sleep of death. But there was his wife, a shimmering presence in the plain's glare. He leapt from his horse and strode over to her. She did not flinch or lower her gaze, and to his amazement he realized that for the first time in his life another person was facing him without fear. For several seconds that stretched to eternity, they sized each other up, trying to gauge the other's strength, and their own powers of resistance. It gradually dawned on both of them that they were up against a formidable opponent. He lowered his gun. She smiled.

Casilda won each moment of the ensuing hours. To all the wiles of seduction known since the beginning of time she added new ones born of necessity to bring this man to the heights of rapture. Not only did she work on his body like an artist, stimulating his every fibre to pleasure, but she brought all the delicacy of her spirit into play on her side. Both knew their lives were at stake, and this added a new and terrifying dimension to their meeting. Nicolas Vidal had fled from love since birth, and knew nothing of intimacy, tenderness, secret laughter, the riot of the senses, the joy of shared passion. Each minute brought the detachment of troops and the noose that much nearer, but he gladly accepted this in return for her prodigious gifts. Casilda was a passive, demure, timid woman who had been married to an austere old man in front of whom she had never even dared appear naked. Not once during that unforgettable afternoon did she forget that her aim was to win time for her children, and yet at some point, marvelling at her own possibilities, she gave herself completely, and felt something akin to gratitude towards him. That was why, when she heard the soldiers in the distance, she begged him to flee to the hills. Instead, Nicolas Vidal chose to fold her in a last embrace, thus fulfilling the prophecy that had sealed his fate from the start.

Translated by Nick Caistor

CUBA

Goodbye Mother

REINALDO ARENAS

1

'Mother's dead,' says Onelia, emerging into the sitting room where we're grimly waiting to take turns at her sickbed. *Dead* she repeats flatly and emphatically. The four of us gape at her, unable to take it in, struck dumb all of a sudden. Solemnly, we line up and file into the big bedroom where she is

2

lying stretched out on the bed; her long body covered up to the neck by the majestic quilt we jointly stitched, under her strict instructions and scrutiny, as a triumphal offering for her last birthday . . . Stiff, for the first time in her life not moving, not watching us, not motioning to us, she lies there. Stiff and white. The four of us tiptoe gingerly over to the bed and stand in silent contemplation. Ofelia bends over her face. Odilia and Otilia, falling to their knees, clasp her feet, while Onelia, going over to the window, gives full vent to her despair. I draw closer to inspect her hard-set features, her tightly pressed lips drawn out in a rictus; I make as if to stroke her face but I'm afraid the sharp edge of her nose will cut my hand. 'Mother, Mother,' Otilia, Odilia, Onelia and Ofelia start to chant. And shrieking and sobbing they circle round her, beating their breasts and brows, tearing their hair, crossing themselves, genuflecting, round and round and round

3

till I too, moaning and pummelling my chest, am drawn into the procession. Utterly disconsolate we continue to wail and gyrate round Mother's body throughout the evening and night, till dawn breaks and it's daylight and still our moans go on. Each time I go past the bedhead I scrutinize her face, which seems to get progressively longer and stranger, till by the following nightfall (which finds us still howling and gyrating) I can hardly recognize her. A ghastly sort of pained, frightened (and frightening) expression has taken possession of her features. I glance up at my sisters. But they, undaunted, unflagging, go on wailing and circling her body, oblivious to the process of change. Mother, Mother, they tirelessly chant, as if possessed, transported into another world. And I follow their gyrations – as another night falls – unable to take my eyes off those ever more discoloured features . . . Mother stripping corn husks, giving out the daily round of orders, filling the night with the smell of coffee, handing round coconut balls, promising we'd all go into town next week: is this the Mother I see before me? Mother tucking us up tight before blowing out the oil-lamp, standing under a tree pissing, riding home in the rain with a bunch of fresh-cut bananas, is this the Mother I see now? Mother summoning us to lunch from the hallway, tall, starched and smelling of herbs, is this what she is now? Mother gathering us together at Christmas time, is this her now? Mother carving the sucking pig, serving the slices of meat, pouring the wine, passing the sweetmeats . . . is this her? Mother (our eyes glued to her) opening up the trap-door and handing down from the loft an array of walnuts, marzipan, candies and dates . . . Is this her? Is this her? Is this her stretched out on the bed before us (it's dawn again), slowly swelling, starting to stink?

4

And, as we keep going round and round, it occurs to me that it's about time we buried her. I break the circle and, slumping down by the closed window, beckon to my sisters. Still wailing, they cluster round me: 'We know how you feel,' Ofelia says, 'but you mustn't give in. You mustn't let your emotions get the better of you. She'd never forgive you . . .' 'Come on,' says Odilia taking me by the hand, 'come with us.' Otilia grasps my other hand: 'She needs us at her side now more than ever.' And so I'm back in the circle, like them wailing, beating my breast with both fists and at times holding my nose . . . And so we carry on (and another night falls). Imperturbable, they halt the procession from time to time to plant a kiss on Mother's disfigured face, clasp one of her bloated hands or smooth back her hair, straighten the folds of her dress, polish her shoes and pull the majestic quilt, now plagued by a swarm of flies, up over her body . . .

Taking advantage of this ritual preening, I too stop as my sisters, engrossed, comb her hair for the umpteenth time, tie a shoelace that has come undone as her feet start to swell, struggle to button up her blouse which her now gigantic bosom keeps popping open. I think, I murmur, head bowed,

5

the time has come to bury her.

6

'Bury Mother!' Ofelia exclaims, while Otilia, Odilia and Onelia look on with an identically shocked expression. 'What's come over you? The thought of burying your own mother . . .!' The four of them glare at me so fiercely that for a moment I think they're going to tear me to pieces. 'Now that she's closer to us than ever! Now that we can stay by her side night and day! Now that she's more beautiful than ever!'

'But haven't you noticed the smell, the flies . . .?'

'How dare you suggest such a thing!' Onelia snaps in my face, flanked by Otilia and Odilia.

'What smell?' says Ofelia. 'How can you bring yourself to say that Mother, our beloved Mother, smells?'

'And who decides what's a good smell and what's a bad smell, anyway?' Ofelia asks. 'Can you say what the difference is?'

I'm lost for words.

'Look at him,' Ofelia goes on. 'The traitor! A traitor to his own mother! To whom we owe everything! To whom we owe our very existence! Unforgivable . . .!'

'Never has she smelt more sweet,' Onelia insists, inhaling deeply.

'What a wonderful, wonderful smell!' Otilia and Odilia chant ecstatically. 'Exquisite!'

They all inhale deeply, glowering at me.

I go over to where Mother is lying; waving aside (for a minute) the clamouring cloud of flies, I too take a deep breath.

7

We are the flies,
delectable and pure
Come and adore us!

Our marvellous bodies are perfectly proportioned
giving us access to any occasion or place.
Funeral or coronation,
wedding cake or bleeding entrails,
there you will find us
cheekily buzzing and flitting, partaking of the spoils.
No festivity do we spare.
No environment do we spurn.
No morsel do we shun.
Watch how we gracefully glide over field and garden
doomed to a fleeting existence.
And yet nothing can stop us
from settling where we like:
on a queen's arse,
on the dictator's nose,
on the fallen hero's wounds, on the suicide's spattered
brains.
Oh come and adore us!
See how prettily we dance, dart and fornicate on the tombs of
the gods of old,
on the rostrum of the latest leader,
swamping the ringing speeches,
soaring above the bowed heads bullied into submission, slipping in between the bound hands bullied into applauding
their own prison sentence.
Look at the fancy coils and carefree whirls we trace over the
sea of skeletons whitening the desert, over the lolling, purple
tongue of the latest victim of the gallows – you!
Look at us buzzing in the ears of the man patiently waiting
his turn in the queue – you?
In the same breath we drink the warm blood of the latest
martyr and feast on the tender heart of the adolescent shot by
the firing squad.
Earthquakes,
explosions,
ice ages and thaws,
ends of eras,
the rise and fall of tyrants.
And we buzz on glorious and undeterred.
Can you name one execution, one massacre, one funeral, one

disaster, one holocaust, one single memorable event
in which we have not played a part?
Watch me go from the dung-hill to the rose.
Look at us on the imperial brow and on the foetus abandoned
in the wood.
In the hallowed halls of the gods I drink my fill and hold my
sway
with the same ease as in the seedy prostitute's haunt.
Oh, name one flower that can vie with us in greatness (in
beauty).
Watch as, after savouring with equal relish the national hero,
the intellectual and the delinquent, we soar heavenward –
pure, calm and regal – to eclipse the sun with our glory.
I challenge you:
Name one flower, just one, that can vie with us in splendour,
in greatness – in beauty.

8

Now the swarm of flies is hovering over Mother's mouth
which – as she enters her second week as a corpse – is gaping
grotesquely while a greyish liquid oozes from her dilated eyes
and nostrils. Her tongue, which has also swollen mons-
trously, lolls out of her mouth (for some inexplicable reason
the flies suddenly take off). Her neck and brow are also
horribly swollen, making her hair stand out at right angles to
her ever more taut skin.

   Odilia comes close and gazes at her.

   'Doesn't she look lovely!'

   'Doesn't she,' I reply.

   We all draw round to admire her.

9

She's exploded. Her face had gone on growing till it turned
into an amazing balloon, and now it's burst. Her stomach,
which had risen so high that the bedspread kept slipping off,
has also burst open. The accumulation of pus sprays us with
its intoxicating perfume. The excrement accumulated in her
bowels also spatters us. The five of us inhale ecstatically.
Hand in hand we start to circle round her once more, gazing
at the strings of mucus and pus hanging from her gaping
nostrils and from her jaw which has now fallen apart. And
her yawning stomach, which has turned into a simmering

morass, starts to emit the most exquisite vapours. Fascinated, we all gather round to watch the spectacle that is Mother. Her intestines bubble and splutter in a series of explosions; the excrement dribbles down her legs – which have also started to bubble and splutter – mingling with the vapours given off by the murky orange-and-green liquid oozing from every pore. Her feet, which have also turned into shiny balloons, burst open inundating our lips as we avidly devour them with kisses. Mother, Mother, we chant as we circle round and round, intoxicated by the exhalations from her heaving body. In the midst of this apotheosis Ofelia suddenly pauses, gazes radiantly at Mother for a few seconds, goes out of the room and

10

here she is back again, brandishing the huge kitchen knife only Mother could (and did) use. 'Now I know what to do!' she cries, interrupting our ceremony. 'Now I know what to do. At last I've deciphered her message . . . Mother,' she goes on turning her back on us and drawing closer, 'here I am, here we are, steadfast and true, ready to obey your every command. Happy to have devoted ourselves and to continue to devote ourselves to you alone, now and for ever . . .' Odilia, Otilia and Onelia also draw near and fall on their knees by the bed, moaning gently. I stay standing by the window. Ofelia ends her speech and goes up to Mother's side. Clutching the huge kitchen knife with both hands she plunges it up to the hilt into her own stomach and, in a frantic flurry of twitching limbs, falls on the sprawling, teeming morass that is now Mother. Otilia's, Odilia's and Onelia's moans rise to a rhythmic crescendo that is intolerable

11

(for me, the only one listening).

12

The wondrous perfume of Mother's and Ofelia's rotting bodies transports us. Both of them are crawling with glistening maggots, and we are riveted to the spot by the spectacle of the transformation process. I look on as Ofelia's corpse, by now in an advanced stage of decomposition, merges with that of Mother to form a single festering, murky mass whose fragrance permeates the whole atmosphere. I also observe the covetous look in Odilia's and Otilia's eyes as they gaze at the heaving mound . . . The odd beetle scuttles in and out of the cavities in either corpse. Right now a rat, tugging at the wondrous heap with all its might, has made off with a piece of flesh (Mother's? Ofelia's?) . . . As if acting on the same impulse, obeying the same command, Otilia and Odilia fling themselves on the remains and – both at the same time – grab the kitchen knife. A brief but violent battle ensues over Mother and Ofelia, sending the magnificent rats scurrying for cover and making the beetles retreat into the mound's innermost recesses. With a deft forward lunge Odilia seizes control of the knife and, clasping it with both hands, makes ready to plunge it into her bosom. But Otilia, breaking free, snatches the weapon away from her. 'How dare you!' she screams at Odilia, stepping on to the heaving mound. 'So you thought you could join her before me, did you? I'll show her I'm the most devoted of the lot.' Before Odilia can stop her, she plunges the knife into her breast and falls on to the heap . . . Whereupon Odilia, in a frenzy, pulls the weapon out of Otilia's chest. 'You selfish bitch! You always were a selfish bitch!' she shrieks at her dying sister. And plunges the knife into her heart, dying (or pretending to die) before Otilia, whose body is still twitching. Both of them eventually expire on top of the mound, locked in a final, furious embrace.

13

We are the rats and the beetles.
Mark our words:
the rats and the beetles.
So come and adore us.
Come and bow down before us,
the only true gods.
Sing hymns of praise to my beetle's body,
a body that in need can feed off its own body,
Dark or light, wet, dry or rough: all paths are ours.
I crawl along the ground but if required I can also fly.
If part of my body gets broken off, it can easily be replaced.
I am self-generating and self-sufficient.
Living off putrefaction, we know the world will be ours for ever.

Liking to build our homes in dark, filthy crannies, we cannot be eliminated from a world made to our measure.
As for us rats,
no praise is high enough for us,
no hymn worthy to be sung in our honour.
Our eyes can see in the dark:
the future is ours.
We can live anywhere,
we have seen all the hells on earth.
There is no sacred text that does not mention us nor apocalypse where we do not appear.
We frequent churches and brothels, the cemetery and the theatre, the teeming city and the primitive hut.
We can swim in rushing waters,
we can disappear into the air.
The world is ours from pole to pole.
We bring life to the castle,
wonder to the graveyard,
we rule the rafters,
we tunnel underground and bring comfort to the prisoner.
We accompany the condemned man both before and after his execution
(living with him, eating with him and then eating him).
We are never still. In sumptuous coffers, in cardboard boxes, on board ship or in the coffin, we march ever onwards.
We are an image of the universal and the eternal.
So we ask not for a crown, which after all is transient,
nor for a nation or a continent, both of which can disappear.
We lay claim to the universe regardless of progress or decay, which is to say that we lay claim to eternity.
I challenge you to name a dove or rose, a fish, eagle or tiger that can boast such talents or make such claims. I challenge you to name any other creature deserving of such epithets.
I challenge you.
As for us beetles, sublime winged creatures that can live underground, in a latrine or in a turret,
we also challenge you to name one flower, one beast, one tree, one god who can equal our greatness and endurance – our capacity for life.

Give us snow or fire,
give us flood or boundless desert.
Put us in solitary confinement or in a crowd.
Subject us to health campaigns or air raids.
Set us on a mountain, on the hard tarmac, in a sealed pipe,
in a ruin,
in a palace or in a pantheon,
in a bottomless pit:
   Oh name me one rose,
     but one rose
that can eclipse my glory.
   Name me one rose,
              but one rose.

14

The fragrance of the rotting bodies of Mother, Ofelia, Odilia and Otilia wafts far and wide, turning the whole area into a delectable wasteland as the horrid birds, the hideous butterflies, the fetid flowers, the pestilent herbs and shrubs, along with the loathsome trees, have vanished or shrivelled up, dying or beating a hasty retreat, shamed (rightly) into submission. Goodbye to all such foul, feeble frivolities. To a vile, idle, unjustifiable landscape. And now the whole area is a magnificent expanse alive with an incredible clamour: the incessant scuttling of rats and beetles, the gnawing of maggots, the tireless hum of iridescent swarms of flies. Swaying to this unrivalled music, intoxicated by this marvellous perfume, Onelia and I go on circling round the enormous mound, and if (just occasionally) we look up it is to contemplate the unstoppable flood of magnificent creatures coming to pay their spontaneous homage: rats, mice and other rodents, splendid outsize beetles, lithe relucent worms. We've thrown open the doors to give them easy access. And still they keep coming. Hordes of them. Whole battalions of them. They mill round our feet in an exuberant, surging tumult, proceeding on to the giant heap over which they swarm to create a mountain in perpetual motion. A dense, billowing, rising, spreading cloud. Constantly changing shape in a singular swaying, shifting, restless, muted frenzy. The grand apotheosis. In homage to Mother. On account of and on behalf of Mother. The grand apotheosis.

With Mother at the centre of it all,
15
reigning supreme, acknowledging the tribute. Waiting
for us.
16
And to join You we go, Onelia and I; still possessing enough
energy (no doubt thanks to Your inspiration) to struggle
towards the mound and, jubilantly, offer ourselves up.
Onelia laboriously clears a pathway through the swarm of
sublime creatures. Pushing aside the busily gnawing rats and
mice, scattering in all directions flies and beetles which
immediately resettle on the spot, plunging her hands into the
swirling mass of maggots, she manages to recover the kitchen
knife. She eyes me warily in case I try to grab it from her. She
lets out a little squeal of triumph and, without further ado,
falls on to the teeming mountain. The stately beetles, the
splendid rats, the sublime scented maggots rearing and
writhing majestically instantly swallow her up.
17
We are the maggots
Come and worship us.
Come and bow down humbly before us, supreme rulers of
the universe, with due reverence, pomp and circumstance
heed our brief but indisputable oration:
Centuries and centuries of toil: all for our benefit.
Millennia and more millennia: and all for our benefit.
Infamous and treacherous deeds,
pride and ambition, castles, towers, royal insignia,
skyscrapers, pageants and
air raids
          bomb blasts,
one swindle after another: all for our benefit.
experiments, congresses,
infiltrators,
slaves and new forms of slavery, elections and other abomi-
nations,
coronations and self-investitures,
revolutions and revolutions betrayed:
crucifixions, scourges, purges and expulsions: all for our
benefit

For just one minute halt your crowing, your bowing and
scraping, your toasts and your condemnations, and pay us
the homage we deserve. Admire
our magnificent figures. We are philosophy, logic, physics
and metaphysics. Moreover we possess an admirable ancient
skill: the art of slithering.
How can we be mutilated when we have no limbs?
Who would think of banishing us when we are the lords of
the subsoil?
Who would want to gouge out our eyes when we have no
need of them?
If we are cut in half we reproduce ourselves.
Who can give us a sense of guilt when we know that in the
dustbin of history all bodies taste the same and all hearts
stink?
What god can damn us (much less destroy us) when dam-
nation is our reason for existence, when
destruction is what gives us life? How can we be devoured if,
after they have devoured us,
we shall end up devouring the devourers?
Fly, beetle, rat: no matter how great your triumphs, they end
at the point where I begin to tunnel my way to power.
How can you destroy me if destruction is the source of my
supremacy?
Where can you run to that my legless, wingless body will not
find you,
where my armless body will not embrace you,
where my mouthless body will not eat you?
Surrender then, surrender.
            I heard you compare yourselves
to roses and to gods.
Do I have to compare myself to such shortlived creatures in
order to sing my praises?
Frankly I loathe hackneyed comparisons, easy victories, fore-
gone conclusions.
So away with you till the moment of sacrifice,
carry on with the circus, keep dancing and prancing,
make merry, hang someone, go for each other's throat.
Invent new swindles and take advantage of old ones,
mortify your neighbour and, if you get the chance,

get fat

get fat

get fat.

The supreme irony: although of all the creatures in the world you and I are the only ones that can be quite certain we'll meet again, I can't in all honestly say *see you later*.

18

The moment has come. The big moment when I must join Mother. Must? Did I say *must*? Want to, *want*, that's the word. And now at last I can by plunging into the seething mass of vermin ... *vermin*? How can such a word have escaped my lips? Can my mother, my beloved mother, that heaving mound, be called *vermin*? Is vermin the word for those sublime creatures awaiting me, to whom I must sacrifice myself? But what am I doing saying *must* again? How can I be so unworthy, how can I forget that it's not a matter of duty but an honour, a spontaneous gesture, a privilege ... Clutching the huge knife in my hands I circle the funeral mound which heaves and contracts and palpitates under the sea of vermin ... That's the second time I've caught myself saying *vermin*! How can I stand here without ripping my tongue out? The overpowering joy of knowing that soon I shall form part of that fragrant heap is evidently making me talk gibberish. Quick, I mustn't (mustn't?) waste another minute. Every passing minute is a mark of my cowardice. My sisters have all joined Mother already, in a marvellous symbiosis. And here am I still circling the funeral mound clutching the kitchen knife in both hands, too much of a coward to plunge it into my chest in one bold thrust. What are you waiting for? I halt next to the sacrificial victims. But what am I doing calling them *sacrificial victims*? So then, I halt beside the mound composed of my beautiful, sweet, selfless, slaughtered sisters. But what villainy is this? How can I use a word like *slaughtered*? I halt beside the mound composed of my four joyfully offered-up sisters. I grasp the knife as firmly as I can and raise it to my chest. I press it against me. But it won't go in. All these weeks of circling the mound without anything to eat must have sapped my strength. But I've got to go through with it. I've got to try again. I've got to make an end of it ... I go into the sitting room which is likewise permeated by the fragrance of Mother and of my sisters. I open the door into the hall, which had blown shut. I place the knife between the frame and the door, pulling the latter to so that the blade is left firmly wedged in place, sticking out at a right angle ready for me to hurl myself on to it and impale myself without any need for muscle power. Just like a character I once saw in a movie I sneaked off to see in town without Mother knowing . . . I remember exactly what happened: the character placed the knife between the frame and the door. He pulled it to. And then he committed suicide by hurling himself on to it. Without, of course, leaving his fingermarks on the weapon . . . What was the film called? And what was the name of the star . . .? The beautiful woman accused of the crime . . . was she his wife . . .? But what am I doing thinking of such trivia when Mother is next door in the bedroom waiting for me. Calling me to join her and all my sisters. I must go . . . Ingrid Bergman! Ingrid Bergman! Now I remember . . . That was the star's name. But what is all this, what on earth are you saying? Ingrid Bergman! Ingrid Bergman! But how dare you utter such words . . .? I open the door and the knife falls to the ground. Outside, beyond the dusty expanse that once was the farmyard and corral – our land – a clump of trees stands out faintly against the distant skyline. I turn round for a moment. Inside I can hear the assorted vermin gnawing away. I go back to contemplate the scene . . . Ingrid Bergman! Ingrid Bergman! I shout the words still louder, drowning the crunching and munching of the rats and other creatures. Ingrid Bergman, Ingrid Bergman, I keep on shouting as I rush out into the open and run across the corral, across the vast expanse of flattened earth till I reach the edge of the wood . . . The stench of the trees fills me with delight; so too the putrescence of the grass in which I roll. Ingrid Bergman! Ingrid Bergman! I'm intoxicated by the rank scent of the roses. I'm an irremediable degenerate. I can't resist the open countryside's corrupting influence. Ingrid Bergman! I flagellate myself, I beat my breast. But I stagger on through the wood, hurtling into the tree trunks, clutching at the leaves, inhaling the fetid fragrance of the lilies of the valley . . . I get to the sea and, stripping off all my clothes, breathe in the salt air. Naked I plunge into the waves which must surely smell nauseous. I forge my way through the no doubt pestilent foam. Ingrid Bergman! Ingrid Bergman! And I dive headlong into the translucent white – stinking? – surf . . . I'm a traitor. A confirmed traitor. And happy.

Translated by Jo Labanyi

GUATEMALA

Woman in the Middle

ARTURO ARIAS

The descent was slow, slow the arriving at the maize-field. From one side to the other, one side to the other of the zigzag track. They never stopped. They hurried along, one side to the other. So they wouldn't feel the weight that was growing heavier and heavier. The weight on their backs, and the other one. The one burning in their insides like an incandescent gas. The one they could sense somewhere in the irregular band of shade that the trees threw on the dry grass. The three of them terror-struck, the weight of their children on their backs. Feliciana thought she was going crazy. She was barefoot, but her feet had ceased to exist for her. Her face swollen from being unable to cry, my God, from being unable to cry. Side to side down the hill.

Shots. They heard them close by, as if they came from the gully, down among the welcoming warmth of the trees. The silence that followed made the foliage tremble. The wind shook twigs and leaves. Her heart was a bloodstained bird fallen in the grass. Another burst of gunfire, the sound gone in an instant like a vanishing swarm of gnats, then the smell of cordite wafted up to her. She rubbed her cheek, as though in need of the rough feel of her premature wrinkles. All of a sudden, the clouds parted. The joy of the sun flooded her.

She raised her hand in an empty gesture. Manuela went out of sight round the next bend. She didn't, couldn't hear Magdalena, lying prone in the ditch by the roadside at the exit to the village. She felt she was inside a huge bubble. Her frightened gaze sought out the river, visible in the distance, south of the bend in the track. She wanted to be reassured that at least one thing was still in its proper place. Yes, there the river was, skeleton-like, silent, empty of people, stretched out under the forlorn desolation of the heart of the sky.

The sun vanished again. She bit on the dry dust that the slightest of breezes had deposited in her mouth, as on the black branches of the pines. She looked up. The clouds resembled enormous black hounds whose four fangs, hungry for flesh, spread over all the landscape, stretched as far as the horizon in pursuit of nameless, innumerable prey. The damp but dusty breeze was like a dog's panting, the warm breath of death unleashed. The hunters were closing in. She speeded up; the colours and textures of the gully quivering like those of a deep lake shimmering nervously. She could feel drops of sweat dripping from her dishevelled hair. She didn't dry herself. She let them moisten her skin, as if in their slow, salty trickling there might be a way to hold back the scream tearing at her from inside: Magdalena lying in the ditch, her unending cry.

A round face. Small eyes, dry from so much sadness. Fleshy, wide nose. What had once been a sturdy body now seemed gaunter with every minute of her descent, one side to the other, with a load so heavy she was beyond feeling it. The sun, the heart of the sky, on her blouse embroidered in yellow, green, violet and orange, lifted one bundle to help lighten her burden. She screwed up her eyes to see into the distance. Though there had been no more sound of shots, she could see all the animals fleeing the woods.

In front of her went Manuela. She appeared, disappeared. She had broken into a trot out of fear. Behind her was only Rosenda. Just her, no one else. But she felt the whole village pressing on her heels. As though all of them had got out of that pit and could begin again. Magdalena, prone in the ditch. Everything was reduced to a memory now. She touched her face, to make sure once more she was still alive. She was. But her memories were a jumble. Everything was mixed up, blanketed in mist. Grey, seeping in everywhere. The dry earth stirred beneath her feet, but could no longer convey anything to her. Now the earth was dry, stripped of maize. Panting from running, sweat coursing all down her body. Inside, nothing left except fear.

Faster. Not from the weight now, but because she couldn't bear to breathe that incandescent gas a moment longer. The bloodstained bird left her breathless. The shadows lengthened, black hounds poised in ambush. She was worn out, lined, weary from the trek. She wanted to wipe away the sweat, but the bundles on her back were so heavy she couldn't risk lifting an arm and overbalancing. She blinked to try to wash out the drops of sweat plucking at her eyes like hungry vultures. Magdalena lying there. The gully was a narrow slit from which to stare up at the sky. The dry dust filling her mouth. She was inside a bubble. The almost dried-up river. Faster. A lizard flashed between her feet, slipped behind a rock. She would have liked to stop and stare at it, but there was no time in their descent that had turned into a fall. Her hands hung heavy. Her whole body was asleep, knocked unconscious. She thought she would never return, there was nothing to return for, she would have to stay for ever in this abyss, listening to her heartbeats, hers alone, until the end of time. Faster, faster.

The river's skeleton was almost directly in front of her. The bend was coming up. She had to shift all the weight over to her left so that her speed didn't topple her to the right and send her off for ever into the dark pit. Dimly, she remembered her mother teaching her this movement. She willed herself to remember, but the only image in her mind was Magdalena. The whole village pressing behind her. Rubber-limbed bodies rolling down into a black pit, savaged by the hounds. Clouds all the time. Cold. Perhaps because of the bloodstained bird. The incandescent gas. Biting on the dry grey dust. No maize. The bend in the track.

She rounded it, and stopped short. Too late to save her from colliding with Manuela's child. The baby's screams wailed on like a siren. Her tiny hands swung through the air, together and apart, together, apart.

Manuela was standing stock still, like a statue. As though she weren't a living being, indistinguishable from the other tree trunks. Craning her neck to peer down into the shadowy depths of the gully. The taste of dust in her mouth. Choking her. The burning load, the ravaging hounds. How she longed to be able to flee along the line of the trees' shadows falling on the dry grass. But her face was too swollen now even to find the heart of the sky. The fangs trying to force the cry from her. It would never end. They had rolled into a pit. The hungry vultures would pluck at her eyes.

The others were climbing the same path. The line of heads grew closer. They were staring up at the women. One after the other, one after the other. Marching up with measured, self-assured steps. She had walked so far, and had reached nowhere. Would never reach anywhere.

From the way they moved and their stripes, they looked like mountain cats. All that was missing were the fangs.

She felt a blow in her back, a jab from an elbow. The siren's wail enveloped her again like a bubble. But the warmth of the scream offered no protection. It was Rosenda, who had run into her just as she had bumped into Manuela. The three of them were trapped. No way for them to retreat. She remembered the ruins of the village. She had been, once. Had been. Everything was finished now. The mountain cats climbing closer, one after the other. Now they were alongside.

Instinctively, she flattened herself against a tree trunk. Manuela and Rosenda did the same. If only she could merge into the foliage, evaporate like the water from the dried-up river, snuff out the embers still burning interminably inside her.

They strode up towards the women, who could hear sobbing. The three of them suppressed their own desire to scream at this boundless silence. They looked at each other, then at the line of soldiers.

She realized something she hadn't noticed before. There were three other women in the middle of the file. She was struck first by their shining eyes and wide mouths. She felt cold, and everything went dark. It couldn't be. How could it possibly be? An explosion shook her ears, her eyes. Fragments of memories flooded back, coloured scraps that dispersed over the dry earth. She felt tainted, pierced by the children's screams. She could barely breathe, as if anticipating a violent blow. Unspeaking. Only the children howled. The file of soldiers right upon them now. Level with them. She didn't want to see.

But she couldn't avoid it, and saw. The three women were being led, their hands tied behind their backs. Two soldiers on either side of them, gripping their arms. Shoving, dragging them along. Their feet traced strange patterns in the dust, leaving long trails which here and there branched out into monstrous shapes that plucked at the eyes. Then again the mist.

The other women were almost surrounded. That was why she had been unable to make them out properly. Everything was unsteady, spinning around her. Things began to loom out of proportion. She wanted to burst out laughing at having felt Magdalena's silence so, as she lay in the ditch at the edge of the village.

She had seen the woman in the middle before. She tried to pretend she didn't recognize her face, because the soldiers were watching her closely, closely. She didn't recognize the face. Yes, this was the first time she had seen her properly, though she might have glimpsed her somewhere before, in a street market perhaps. Before, everything was possible. Before.

Of course, she did recognize the face. It wasn't the first time she had seen her. The woman in the middle, this stranger hemmed in by soldiers and with her hands tied behind her back, this woman was her mother.

The long line continued on its way up the slope, disappeared round the bend. Feliciana stared at the spot where the woman had vanished, but saw only dark undergrowth.

Translated by Nick Caistor

The Proof

RODRIGO REY ROSA

One night while his parents were still on the road returning from someone's birthday party, Miguel went into the living room and stopped in front of the canary's cage. He lifted up the cloth that covered it and opened the tiny door. Fearfully, he slipped his hand inside the cage, and then withdrew it doubled into a fist, with the bird's head protruding between his fingers. It allowed itself to be seized almost without resistance, showing the resignation of a person with a chronic illness, thinking perhaps that it was being taken out so the cage could be cleaned and the seeds replenished. But Miguel was staring at it with the eager eyes of one seeking an omen.

All the lights in the house were turned on. Miguel had gone through all the rooms, hesitating at each corner.

God can see you no matter where you are, Miguel told himself, but there are not many places suitable for invoking Him. Finally he decided on the cellar because it was dark there. He crouched in a corner under the high vaulted ceiling, as Indians and savages do, face down, his arms wrapped around his legs, and with the canary in his fist between his knees. Raising his eyes into the darkness, which at that moment looked red, he said in a low voice: 'If you exist, God, bring this bird back to life.' As he spoke, he tightened his fist little by little, until his fingers felt the snapping of the fragile bones, and an unaccustomed stiffness in the little body.

Then, without meaning to, he thought of María Luisa the maid, who took care of the canary. A little later, when he finally opened his hand, it was as if another, larger hand had been placed on his back – the hand of fear. He realized that the bird would not come back to life. If God did not exist, it was absurd to fear His punishment. The image, the concept of God went out of his mind, leaving a blank. Then, for an instant, Miguel thought of the shape of evil, of Satan, but he did not dare ask anything of him.

He heard the sound of the car going into the garage over his head. Now the fear had to do with this world. His parents had arrived; he heard their voices, heard the car doors slam and the sound of a woman's heels on the stone floor. He laid the inert little body on the floor in the corner, groped in the dark for a loose brick and set it on top of the bird. Then he heard the chiming of the bell at the front door and ran upstairs to greet his parents.

'All the lights on!' exclaimed his mother as he kissed her.

'What were you doing down there?' his father asked him.

'Nothing. I was afraid. The empty house scares me.'

His mother went through the house, turning off lights to right and left, secretly astonished by her son's fear.

That night Miguel had his first experience of insomnia, a word he had never heard. For him not sleeping was a kind of nightmare from which there was no hope of awakening. A static nightmare: the dead bird beneath the brick, and the empty cage.

Hours later Miguel heard the front door open, and the sound of footsteps downstairs. Paralysed by fear, he fell asleep. María Luisa the maid had arrived. It was seven o'clock; the day was still dark. She turned on the kitchen light, set her basket on the table and, as was her custom, removed her sandals in order not to make any noise. She went into the living room and uncovered the canary's cage. The little door was open and the cage was empty. After a moment of panic, during which her eyes remained fixed on the cage hanging in front of her, she glanced around, covered the cage again and returned to the kitchen. Very carefully she took up her sandals and the basket, and went out. When she was no longer in sight of the house she put the sandals on and started to run in the direction of the market, where she hoped to find another canary. She had to replace the one which she thought had escaped due to her carelessness.

Miguel's father awoke at quarter past seven. He went down to the kitchen and, surprised to see that María Luisa had not yet come, decided to go to the cellar for the oranges and squeeze them himself. Before going back up to the kitchen, he tried to turn off the light, but his hands and arms were laden with oranges, so that he had to use his shoulder to push the switch. One of the oranges slipped from his arm and rolled across the floor into a corner. He pushed the light on once more. Placing the oranges on a chair, he made a bag out of the front of his dressing-gown, dropped them into it, and went to pick up the orange in the corner. And then he noticed the bird's wing sticking out from under the brick. It was not easy for him, but he could guess what had happened. Everyone knows that children are cruel, but how should he react? His wife's footsteps sounded above him in the kitchen. He was ashamed of his son, and at the same time he felt that they were accomplices. He had to hide the shame and the guilt as if they were his own. He picked up the brick, put the bird in his dressing-gown pocket and climbed up to the kitchen. Soon he went on upstairs to his room to wash and dress.

A little later, as he left the house, he met María Luisa returning from the market with the new canary hidden in her basket. She greeted him in an odd fashion, but he did not notice it. He was upset: the hand that he kept in his pocket held the bird in it.

As María Luisa went into the house she heard the voice of Miguel's mother on the floor above. She put the basket on the floor, took out the canary, and ran to slip it into the cage, which she then uncovered with an air of relief and triumph. But then, when she drew back the curtains and the sun's rays tinted the room pink, she saw with alarm that the bird had one black foot.

It was impossible to awaken Miguel. His mother had to carry him into the bathroom, where she turned on the tap and with her wet hand gave his face a few slaps. Miguel opened his eyes. Then his mother helped him dress and get down the stairs. She sat him down at the kitchen table. After he had taken a few swallows of orange juice, he managed to rid himself of his sleepiness. The clock on the wall marked quarter to eight; shortly María Luisa would be coming in to get him and walk him to the corner where the school bus stopped. When his mother went out of the room, Miguel jumped down from his chair and ran down into the cellar. Without turning on the light he went to look for the brick in the corner. Then he rushed back to the door and switched on the light. With the blood pounding in his head, he returned to the corner, lifted the brick and saw that the bird was not there.

María Luisa was waiting for him in the kitchen. He avoided her and ran to the living room. She hurried after him. When on entering the room he saw the cage by the window, with the canary hopping from one perch to the other, he stopped short. He would have gone nearer to make certain, but María Luisa seized his hand and pulled him along to the front door.

On his way to the factory where he worked, Miguel's father was wondering what he would say to his son when he got home that night. The road was empty. The weather was unusual: flat clouds like steps barred the sky, and near the horizon there were curtains of fog and light. He lowered the window, and at the moment when the car crossed a bridge over a deep gully he took one hand off the steering wheel and tossed the bird's tiny corpse out.

In the city, while they waited on a corner for the bus, María Luisa listened to the account of the proof Miguel had been granted. The bus appeared in the distance, in miniature at the end of the street. María Luisa smiled. 'Perhaps that canary isn't what you think it is,' she said to Miguel in a mysterious voice. 'You have to look at it very close. If it has a black foot, it was sent by the Devil.' Miguel stared into her eyes, his face tense. She seized him by the shoulders and turned him around. The bus had arrived; its door was open. Miguel climbed on to the platform and looked behind him. 'Dirty witch!' he shouted.

The driver started up. Miguel ran to the back of the bus and sat down by the window in the back row. There was the squeal of tyres, a horn sounded, and Miguel conjured up the image of his father's car.

At the last stop before the school the bus took on a plump boy with narrow eyes. Miguel made a place for him at his side.

'How's everything?' the boy asked him as he sat down.

The bus ran between the rows of poplars, while Miguel and his friend spoke of the vast power of God.

Translated by Paul Bowles

MEXICO

Martina's Wardrobe

JESÚS GARDEA

The boat nearly sank from the weight as the wardrobe tilted dangerously, reflecting the sun and the dirty waters of the lake in its mirror. The men who had lifted it aboard sprinted out of the water and up the muddy beach. Their shouts of panic drew jeers from the curious onlookers who were watching them load. But they ignored the insults, and once they were on safe ground, turned to see what was happening to the boat. The wardrobe was still swaying back and forth, its high carved pediment waving in the morning light. The owner of the boat had stayed in the water, expecting the worst. To damage a piece of furniture like that would mean ruin for him. It had happened often enough in the past to other owners with other loads. Then everyone by the lakeside saw the colour return to his face as his nerves calmed. Some of them clapped. The boatman lifted an arm in acknowledgement, then shouted for the deserters to come back to him. A woman at the lakeside carrying a bottle of water stopped one of them and offered it him. Grasping it by the neck, he held it up against the sunlight, and shook it gently. 'Why are you doing that?' the woman wanted to know. (The boatman was still calling them back.) 'To make sure there's nothing in the water,' he replied. Then he turned his back on her and strode off across the mud. Soon the men's voices were heard again from the lake.

They clustered round the boat. They still had to centre the wardrobe properly, to make sure it was balanced so that the swell of the water would not topple it during the crossing. Slowly, cautiously, they reached out to the shiny mahogany. 'If your hands are sweaty, don't touch,' the boatman warned. 'Let the air dry them off first.' It was his task, with three others, to hold on to the wardrobe and keep it steady, in between the main oars. The boatman could see his own face

81

and his glowing bald patch reflected in the polished wood. The sight amused him. He grimaced in fake annoyance, then grinned, showing gums as bare as hills. He pulled another face. The men were impatient for him to have done with his fooling about: the water was freezing their legs.

It was past noon by the time they could rest on some rocks by the lakeside. The boat owner drank the water from the bottle without once taking his eyes off the wardrobe. When he'd finished, he rammed the bottle into the mud by his side, resting one hand on it.

'So you don't know who the woman was, Cristóbal?' he asked his companion who had brought the water.

'That I don't, Don Arnulfo.'

'You mean you didn't bother to take a good look at her?'

'Maybe not . . .'

'Did she say anything?'

'Not a thing. But I don't think she liked me checking the water.'

'You could have done that here, with us.'

'I won't say you're wrong, Don Arnulfo.'

'Well then, Cristóbal?'

'The poison. Don't forget, the more powerful it is, the quicker it dissolves.'

'I don't forget anything.'

'Ah, but sometimes you do, Don Arnulfo.'

The boat owner pulled the bottle from the mud and gulped the rest down.

The men followed him into the village, fanning themselves with their straw hats. Under a blue awning outside a store they met up with the man who had arranged for them to carry the load. They stopped their fanning and greeted him all together. He returned their greeting, throwing his arms wide as though to embrace each and every one of them. 'See you afterwards,' he shouted to the owner. It was a long street, and the house they were headed for was at the top end.

An old man, barefoot and naked from the waist up, opened the door.

'We're looking for Martina Carrasco,' the boatman said.

'Martina Carrasco isn't here,' the old fellow said.

'Where is she?'

'Couldn't say.'

'When will she be back?'

'Couldn't tell you that either.'

'She owes us money.'

'She owes the whole world money.'

'We've loaded her wardrobe on to the boat.'

'That makes no odds.'

'Yes, it makes odds. If that wardrobe is left out at the mercy of the weather it'll be ruined, and it's a fine piece of furniture.'

'Martina Carrasco is in debt in all weathers.'

'We'll wait for her anyway.'

'You'll be grilled by the sun. Come back later.'

'We're used to the sun.'

'There's no telling when she'll be back.'

'Then we'll wait for her in the store where they sell beer. Tell her that. And tell her we're not crossing the lake until she pays us something.'

The man had gone from under the awning. A stack of empty beer cans stood on the ice-box. The boatman picked up the top one and shook it: 'Still got some,' he said, putting it to one side. He tried another: 'Still got some,' he repeated. Only six of the cans were of any interest to him. He poured all the dregs into one, then, raising it like a glass, waved it in a toast to the men, who were standing in the sun. He finished off the beer in two noisy gulps, then belched in the direction of the store doorway.

'Hey, Cristóbal.'

'Yes, Don Arnulfo.'

'Ask them inside where we can find our man.'

'How will they know, Don Arnulfo?'

'Everybody knows everybody in this village.'

'Yes.'

The boatman crushed the can between his thumbs. The men stood staring at him.

'Don Arnulfo, inside they say they don't know, but that he's easy enough to find.'

'And what's the man's name, Cristóbal?'

'I couldn't say.'

'Didn't you ask them, Cristóbal?'

'No, Don Arnulfo.'

'Go back in and ask then.'

They walked back up the street again. The sun, beating on the earth under their feet, raised clouds of dust that concealed their steps. The town was dead. The whitewash on the housefronts was sizzling. From behind shut doors and windows came the sound of distant voices, like those of people groping their way along a mountain ledge. Sleepy birds the size of crows drowsed on the parapets. The noise of the men fanning themselves with their hats disturbed the birds briefly, but almost at once they fell back into sleep, twitching their hooked beaks. The boatman trudged along wearily, dulled by the dazzling white walls and the effects of the beer.

'Tell me something, Cristóbal.'

'What's that, Don Arnulfo?'

'What's become of all the people who cheered my courage this morning?'

'I don't see them anywhere, Don Arnulfo.'

'Perhaps they weren't from these parts, Cristóbal.'

'Maybe so, Don Arnulfo.'

The whole group marched up to the house door. 'You can't all knock at once,' the boatman said. 'Cristóbal, you get the old man out here.' The stone struck the door with a hollow, resounding thud. The men all instinctively put their hands over their ears. All along the rooftops, the birds ruffled their feathers. 'Not so loud, Cristóbal,' the boatman said. 'There are people at home, and birds asleep, and peaceful fish in the lake.'

'What about Doña Martina?' Cristóbal asked the old man.

'I already told you, she's not here.'

'Hasn't she come back yet?'

'I told you, she only gets back late.'

'What about the other one?'

'What other one?'

'The other Carrasco.'

'Which Carrasco?'

'Gertrudis.'

'What do you want with him?'

'Is he here?'

'Why here? There's more than one Carrasco in the village.'

'They told us in the store that Gertrudis is Martina's husband. We saw him when we first came up here. He was drinking beer under the awning.'

'Does he owe you money?'

'No. He was the one who hired us to take the wardrobe. It was already by the lakeside, all we had to do was load it on to our boat. But he told us that a woman here, in this house, would pay us for taking it.'

'You shouldn't have listened to him.'

'Why not? There's not much work, and lots of competition. All the others have motorboats. And someone has already tried to get rid of our boss Arnulfo by poisoning him.'

'You shouldn't have listened to Gertrudis. It isn't Martina's wardrobe.'

'Whose is it then?'

'God knows. It appeared this morning on the shore, its mirror gazing at the waters of the lake.'

Translated by Nick Caistor

The Trip

MARÍA LUISA PUGA

'We're nothing but a mass of contradictions,' he was saying, just as we met the lorry and felt the rush of wind buffeting our tiny Volkswagen. It was a narrow road and neither vehicle had slowed down. The word 'contradictions' hung in the air for a second. I thought: 'That's what we are all right.' But then what? What are we to make of it, I was wondering, at the same time sensing we weren't on the road any more, though we were still following the route it traced perfectly calmly.

'What then?' I asked.

'Well . . .' and by now we were coasting along some distance from the road, chatting away despite the oppressive midday heat, resigned to the miles that still lay between us and Mexico City '. . . you simply have to accept them.'

Aha? So all one had to do was to accept them? Recognize them, identify them, then leave them be? Take them seriously, pay them attention . . . that seemed fair enough, as we glided towards the green hills. I couldn't understand why E. was bothering to steer round the bends or change down, when we were floating along so serenely.

'That's odd,' L. commented from the back. 'We've left the road.'

'The best thing to do,' A. recommended,' is to try not to think about it. To let yourself go. Otherwise, things may turn out far worse.'

I didn't believe him. His tone of voice – I couldn't believe it. It was cold, not dispassionate. I could tell he was as disconcerted as me. As all of us, probably.

'Of course,' said E. 'It's not so hard. Simply try not to see yourself in any exact location. Let yourself go.'

'Like we are doing now,' said L. though it sounded more like a question than a statement.

'Correct,' A. agreed. 'Anyway, there's nothing else we can do.'

'Well, if you say so, you must be right; but I can't help feeling there's something odd in all this,' I insisted, glancing out of the car window.

E. was driving along at a leisurely pace, listening, but absorbed in his own thoughts. We all had things to do in the city, so we were happy to drift along, in no hurry to arrive.

L. was the only one who still seemed to find it strange that we had left the road. 'I don't know about the rest of you, but this looks weird to me. The trees seem so close.'

'That's what's nice about it,' E. said. 'You mean to tell me you don't like them?'

'If you look closely,' A. pointed out, 'you can see they all have different expressions. Have you noticed? That one over there is so solemn, for example.'

I couldn't see which one he meant. I wasn't particularly looking for it. I wasn't so much interested in our surroundings as in the new state we found ourselves in, which seemed to have something to do with those contradictions. All the same, it was impossible not to notice that we were getting further and further from any point of reference, that is, the road.

'Where is this leading us?' L. wanted to know, but the question seemed completely inappropriate.

'Wherever you wish,' E. reassured her. 'It's for you to choose.'

'I'm fine,' A. said. 'I'm happy to carry on as we are.'

'Me too,' I lied.

'What about you, L.?' E. asked.

'I feel ill, a bit sick, but don't let that worry you.'

'Where were we then? Anyone remember?'

'Contradictions,' I said. 'What colour are they, do you reckon?'

'Red, of course, though sometimes they have brownish tinges.'

'No, they're blue,' L. put in.

'Trust a Pisces to be so categorical,' A. said. 'Don't listen to her.'

'No, I don't think they're blue at all,' I objected, staring at the horizon. 'That doesn't sound right.'

'No? Well, red and brown it is then. Here and there. Nothing's nothing,' he chuckled. 'I mean, none of them is entirely one thing, is it?'

'Agreed. I am though,' A. said.

'I'm trying to get a picture of them,' I said, not yet convinced. 'Or could it be I have never acknowledged them before? How are you feeling, L.?'

'Actually, I don't feel at all well. I'd like to get out for a while, if that's possible.'

E. studied her face in his rear-view mirror. Then he looked to his left, slowed down and said, rather bewildered: 'I'm not sure we can stop here.'

'I'm not sure we can stop, period,' I corrected him.

'Try to hang on, L.; it's too complicated to stop right now,' A. said.

'OK, but how much further is it?'

'I've lost all notion,' E. admitted.

'Why can't we pull up near that hill over there? What d'you say, E.?'

'Yes, I wouldn't mind stretching my legs.'

'Great idea,' said L.

The car began a gentle descent. E. was steering with one hand, stroking his moustache thoughtfully with the other. He pulled up beside a tree and switched off the car engine. He sat for a while before opening the door.

'Right,' he said with a yawn. 'Here we are. Who's for a little stroll?'

All of us.

Such a strange sensation to stand up. To stretch one's legs, feel oneself walking, to look around. I was trembling, but it wasn't an unpleasant feeling, simply a new one.

'What time is it, by the way?' A. asked.

For a moment, I had to think hard what the question meant. I had to try to imagine what A. could possibly need to make him ask such an extraordinary question as: 'what time is it?' I saw E. glancing at his watch, and recalled a similar gesture on my part. L. was leaning against the car boot, gazing out absent-mindedly as though she hadn't heard A. E. and I replied in the same breath: 'My watch has stopped.'

'That's strange, so has mine. That's why I was asking . . .'

'Where are we?' L. butted in.

'I couldn't say for sure, but I reckon we must be about half way there, don't you? How long is it since we left Cuautla?'

We were all struck speechless. Cuautla. When on earth had we been in Cuautla?

'I used to go to Cuautla when I was a little girl . . . I went once with my parents,' I volunteered.

'I go more often,' E. said. 'My folks have a house there, but I haven't been in months.'

'You were the one who brought it up,' L. put in. 'It's the first time I've ever heard the word "Cuautla".'

'You must have heard of Cuautla. Remember, you have to cross it to reach Cuernavaca.'

'For all those who know . . . the shape . . . of things to come, here on WFM,' came faintly from the car radio.

'We went to Cuernavaca six months ago, on that other trip, didn't we?'

'No, it was before that.'

'What a strange place this is,' L. murmured.

'Why?' I wanted to know.

'It looks to me as if none of the greenery has any stems. Look at the grass, the trees.'

I took a good look round. All I could see was green. Green everywhere, shapeless, dense, unending.

'What do you mean, the stems? I don't get you.'

'Just look at the grass. It's completely flat on the ground. Look at the leaves on the trees. I've never seen anything like it.'

In the distance, the trees seemed weighed down by their exuberant foliage. A green swelling in the skirts of the hills. L. was right, the grass did seem like a cloak of moss stretched out on the earth. Nothing stood out. It was as if everything was lying flat, featureless, though the colour was extraordinarily deep and intense. The land was like a padded mattress. Suddenly I noticed another strange thing: the horizon had vanished. We were entirely surrounded by the flat green plain, which gave way in the distance to equally green hills.

'Hey,' I called to E. 'This is really a weird place, isn't it?' I tried to point into the distance, realizing as I did so that I was searching for the dividing line between earth and sky. My hand traced a circle, inviting the others to follow it. E. obligingly did so. 'It's beautiful,' he said.

L.'s jaw had dropped. 'I'd like to move on now,' she suggested.

E. looked sad. Then he looked at me and said: 'How come the four of us can never really be together? If it's not one, then it's another: there's always someone who wants to be off, who puts an end to the moment . . .'

'And that's with just four of us. Imagine what it's like with a whole society.'

We all laughed, but our expressions had changed. I could sense the difference in my own by looking at the others'. They were all pale, anxious. All of them peering nervously around. I stared at them (probably too much of a coward to look at what they might be looking at). But their faces gave me some indication of what must be happening to me.

'What shall we do now?' I asked E.

'Move on, I guess – what else?'

So easy, of course, to get back into the car and drive off. But suddenly I for one couldn't imagine the car or any idea of leaving. It was all so crazy, so ridiculous, like when you're already in bed, asking: what time shall we go to bed? I decided the others must be playing a trick, so I started to laugh. Then they all joined in, peals of laughter, doubled up, sprawled over the car, toppling on to the grass, wiping away their tears (which only brought twice as many to my eyes). I slipped down with the rest of them, letting myself go in a fit of uncontrollable hilarity that was born as an echo of their laughter. I think that for a split second I thought of the future and how I had missed my last chance of knowing it, but the laughter was pressing so hard inside my chest that as I gave in to it, I had to sadly relinquish a whole host of fresh intentions. Yet that moment when I lay down was exquisite. A real arrival where I belonged. My own place.

'I can hear voices. Someone's coming,' said E.

We'd laughed so much we couldn't sit up.

'You're right,' A. said. 'I can hear them too.'

Then I also heard sounds in the distance, like a happy crowd. It reminded me of when I used to live near a theatre.

The noise the audience made as they left after the last show at two in the morning. I would wake up, and their laughter, their chatter, the sound of car engines, was a gentle disturbance, like someone coming to tuck me in.

'Oh yes,' I said, 'they're leaving the theatre.'

The others burst out laughing.

'Don't cackle like that,' I protested, 'they'll think we're having a party or something.'

That sounded lame even to my own ears. By now the others were writhing on the ground.

'Be quiet, dammit, who will they take us for?'

Idiots. Weeping with mirth. And the people were getting closer. Bringing with them their own noise, from their side. A sudden panic gripped me. 'Please,' I begged the others, 'be a bit quieter, or they'll realize we're here.'

'If they're headed this way it's precisely for that reason, because they've spotted us.'

'It can't be,' I said, more and more terrified. 'We must do something, E., they're almost here.'

'It doesn't matter. They'll understand,' he soothed me.

So then I relaxed and fell silent, laughter still tickling me, but the fun gone. Waiting to hear the simple words:

'Yes, they were all killed, poor souls.'

Translated by Nick Caistor

NICARAGUA

Saint Nikolaus

SERGIO RAMÍREZ

for Dorel

The moment Frau Schleting came towards him, arms out-stretched, to get him to dance, he knew it was the start of the disaster he had feared all evening but now was powerless to avert.

If only he could have taken his hundred-mark fee and left as soon as he had finished his job, by now he would have been back in the dank loneliness of his room, smoking his last Krone before wrapping himself in the quilt that was falling apart at the seams, to go to sleep with no greater fear than that the dull routine of his days would go on unchanged.

The first complication had been the sheer size of the pile of presents. He had spent close to an hour helping the boy unwrap the parcels, and they had still done fewer than half. The child's fascination had given way to disinterest, and he was dozing in the middle of a profusion of toys, wrapping paper, boxes and ribbons when Herr Schleting carried him off to bed.

But that hadn't really been the cause – he might even so have got his money and left the house, walked down into the U-Bahn at Viktorie-Louise-Platz, and have been in his room before it had begun to snow. Yes, he muttered to himself as he listened to the measured but inexorable tread of footsteps coming up the stairs: it was Frau Schleting who had brought on the disaster.

A hundred marks would ease a lot of his worries, he had said to himself the night before when Petrus, the barman in Los Nopales, had suggested the kind of job that anyone in his position would have been glad to accept: there were still a few vacancies for Santa Clauses to go and entertain rich children in their homes on Christmas Eve. Petrus's girlfriend worked in the Kantstrasse employment agency and could arrange everything.

That morning, when he arrived at the agency, she had whispered a warning that this wasn't really a job for foreigners, still less for people who looked Latin American or Turkish: they always preferred white, ruddy-cheeked men. But since she was on his side, she wouldn't mention that at all to them, and gave him the address and telephone number: Barbarossastrasse 19/II, in Wilmersdorf: Herr and Frau Schleting. Ring beforehand to sort out the details.

By noon, he still didn't have a Santa Claus costume, and realized he was going to have to ask Krista if she'd lend him the fifty marks he needed to hire the suit and put down a deposit. When he went to look for her at her work in the tiny basement stationer's shop of the Europa Centre, she had answered in her habitual gruff voice, hoarse from cigarette smoking and thickened still further by her feigned anger, that yes she would lend him the money, but that this was the very last favour she would ever do him.

Fifteen years earlier, when he had arrived in Berlin from Maracaibo to study electrical engineering at the Technical University, thanks to his father's snobbish desire to see his son a graduate engineer from Germany, one of his first misfortunes had been to meet Krista, then working as a cashier in the Goethe Institute.

He never mentioned Krista in the long letters he wrote his father attempting to explain his repeated failures as a student, but if he had to put the blame on anyone, it would have been her, not because she really was the culprit, but simply because she had been a part of his life here from the very beginning. And when eventually he gave up attending the university, and with his father's death had begun to scratch a living as a waiter or a stand-in musician in pizzerias and Latino restaurants, Krista was still around, sitting all alone at her table, slowly sipping her beer (even though lately they scarcely exchanged a word) and slowly wasting away in her pursuit of him.

The tiny costume rental shop in Karl Marxstrasse, in Neuköln, had only one Santa Claus outfit left, which didn't fit him. In recent years he had acquired a paunch just like his father's, the suit was far too tight, even though he imagined Santa Clauses ought to be decidedly rotund, which he certainly wasn't. The red flannel trouser legs left a wide expanse of calf exposed, and worse still, the boots weren't included in the outfit, so he would have to turn up in his worn-out winter shoes.

But finally, hours earlier on this Christmas Eve, he had donned the costume and walked down the stairs of the nondescript, grey building identical to so many others along the Manitusstrasse in the outlying workers' district of Kreuzberg, overrun these days by Turkish immigrants, who crowded the streets gesticulating like characters in silent movies and set up their stalls on the pavements or under the bridges.

His footsteps echoed like hammer blows down the endless wooden staircase. As he stepped out into the yard, in whose lofty walls only an occasional lighted window shone, gusts of icy wind stung his face beneath the shiny strands of the false beard. Side by side in the darkness of the yard, the frozen rubbish bins resembled a row of tombstones.

Trying hard to conceal the red suit under his overcoat, he had walked along the Maybach Ufer as stealthily as a burglar, but the cold made his hand shake so much that the tinkling of his bell gave him away in spite of himself to the rare passersby who scurried along the street and rushed into the dark doorways. He left behind the black waters of the canal with its reflections of the street lamps in the night still free of snow, and made his way down into the Kottbusser Tör U-Bahn.

The station platform was deserted apart from a tiny, smartly dressed old lady, who at first stared at him in amazement, then smiled pleasantly to show she had understood. He walked past her to the furthest of the brightly lit, empty yellow cars that had just pulled up in front of them with a drawn-out gentle sigh.

The train moved off in the direction of Nollendorf-Platz, where he had to change. As so often before, the giants on the station advertisements flashed in front of him. He knew that, though in the end the passengers were swallowed up by the darkness of the tunnels, *they* remained up there in their multicoloured Valhalla, their confident smiles like disdainful sneers, a constant reminder of how insignificant was his passage through the stations on his daily journeys in those same yellow trains, set against their happy, triumphant permanence high on the walls. Once again he was dazzled by the vision of a girl with magnificent hair smoking a cigarette, the same girl who through the days of summer, when a clinging smell of dog shit filled the Berlin air, stared defiantly out at the world as she hung from the rigging of a white yacht. Now, as he slipped into the tunnel, she had on a pair of skis and was looking haughtily out from a perfect, snowy landscape, so bursting with happiness her eyes were gleaming mercilessly: *gut gelaunt geniessen.*

He felt for the packet of Krone inside the Santa Claus jacket that reeked of mothballs. A cough followed in the lonely train car, his chronic racking cough from all those icy winters. He was down to his last three cigarettes. He felt for them simply to reassure himself they still existed, that they hadn't already become part of his past, because until the night before he had been getting a packet of Krone every day in Los Nopales out of the money he earned playing the drums for the Caribbean group that appeared there.

Los Nopales was a dive in Carmenstrasse frequented by students. In spite of its name, the only thing Mexican about it was a dusty wide-brimmed sombrero pinned to a Mexican blanket over the bar. The previous evening the police had closed the place down for reasons of hygiene, and Petrus, as he was paying him off, had handed him a final packet of Krone together with a few marks. There's no chance of you lot working as Santa Clauses, Petrus had joked to the Caribbean musicians as they snapped shut their instrument cases in the gloom and made their way out through the kitchen door. The blacks had all shaken their heads, highly amused.

The shops in the Viktorie-Louise-Platz loomed in the darkness, their neon lights extinguished on this silent Christmas Eve. As he crossed the rough cobbles of the square trying to find Barbarossastrasse, he could feel both his toes poking out of the holes in the thick pair of socks. A wave of anger swept over him at the scratchy false beard, at his nagging cough, at this absolute certainty that he would never return to Maracaibo. His father's death, which meant an end to the stream of letters that had brought him good humour, enthusiasm, a never-failing cheque and an unswerving optimism that one day he would be an engineer despite the passing of the years, also meant that all his connections with his family had ceased, apart from an occasional letter from his two sisters, who were married to genuine engineers. They wrote to him, with a mixture of affection and scorn, as 'the German', in a distant echo of his father's former cheerfulness.

Then when he had rung the doorbell, he met Herr Schleting, impeccably dressed in a black dinner suit, the very image of one of those mature, dignified giants who advertised Jägermeister brandy: *Der Deutsche mit dem freundlichen Akzent*. Over his shoulder he could see, not a wretched evil-smelling hole like his own, with books piled in heaps in the corners, rolls of useless plans, and tourist posters of Venezuela as the only decoration, but instead a supernaturally lit living room, just like those of the billboard giants, a seemingly endless mansion whose spaciousness was extended infinitely by mirrors, white walls, crimson curtains, marble fireplaces, and crystal chandeliers, statuettes, flower vases, standard lamps, a vast expanse of carpet: and all this set out as exquisitely as in the Möbel Grünewald ad: *die altmodische Neumode*.

Cautious and diffident, Herr Schleting had smiled and ushered him in with a curt nod of the head. Precisely as they had agreed over the telephone, the little boy was waiting for him seated on the red velvet armchair next to the massive fireplace that had more the air of an altar. Quiet but expectant, wearing a blue corduroy suit, the child must have been given instructions not to budge from the huge pile of blue, red, and gold boxes, which towered almost as high as the glittering Christmas tree.

Herr Schleting had exclaimed, with festive solemnity: 'Santa Claus! Santa Claus!' and stepped back so that he could begin; but he stood hesitating on the doorstep in stunned bewilderment, not knowing how to start, confronted by the apparition of the boy on his distant throne in the centre of this huge advertising poster.

He couldn't recall how or why he had started to laugh strenuously and fling his arms up and down like the toy Santa Clauses in the stores, as the occasion demanded, with every gesture sneaking a look at Herr Schleting, who still stood, smiling imperturbably, in the open doorway. He swaggered over to the boy, at last remembering to ring his bell, and hearing his own deep-throated false laughter as if the sound took a long while to emerge from his throat, where it was a struggle as to whether his wheezing cough or the guffaws would win out.

It was some time later that Frau Schleting had made her appearance. By then he had already started to help the boy unwrap his presents, throwing in the occasional chortle, when suddenly he heard the strains of 'Stille Nacht, Heilige Nacht' blaring out. It was then that he had seen her, dancing alone as if in a dream, waving a bottle of Mumm in one hand, a glass high over her head in the other, as she swayed to the rhythm. She was oblivious to Santa Claus's triumphant arrival and to the ceremony of the presents. Just as in the Mumm advertisements, she was dressed in a long, white lace gown, low-cut at the back, her neck and wrists bedecked with jewels: *Mumm, reicher Genuss entspringt der Natur*.

Herr Schleting had gone discreetly over to turn the music down, then returned to his vantage point for the opening of the presents, but Frau Schleting insisted on turning it up again, and went on dancing, bottle in hand. Finally it was Herr Schleting who gave up and allowed her to continue with her Christmas cheer.

When the boy had become drowsy, Herr Schleting motioned politely for him to stop. He asked him to take a seat for a moment while he put his son to bed. All this time Frau Schleting carried on spinning around the room without paying him the slightest attention. She drank from her glass of Mumm, and by now was clapping to the beat of a Bavarian brass band that had replaced the carol.

On his return, Herr Schleting had asked him sombrely if he would care for anything to drink and he, spluttering through the troublesome strands of the false beard, had answered automatically that he'd like a beer, not really sure he wanted a drink at all, but feeling that a beer would be the most modest and respectful thing to ask for in all that glittering luxury.

Herr Schleting pulled the green bottle from his sleeve like a magician and ceremoniously poured the Kronbacher out into a long-stemmed glass, much weightier in his hand than it had appeared. Somewhere beyond the glass where the golden beer shone, *mit Felsquellwasser gebraut*, was a greeny-blue pond sketched hazily behind a bank of reeds that swayed gently in the breeze.

Herr Schleting stood, his arms folded in front of him, looking on with the detached air of a scientist as he waited for him to finish his drink. He was swallowing it down as quickly as he could, convinced that as soon as he stood up Herr Schleting would whisk a gold-edged leather wallet from his dinner jacket pocket and hand him a brand-new, crisp, hundred-mark note.

With what in all likelihood were intended as his parting words, Herr Schleting had then asked him – pronouncing each word slowly and distinctly as people do when trying to be polite to foreigners, where exactly he came from. How extraordinary! he had said with a hollow laugh, he hadn't spotted his accent at all on the telephone: as if rather than being a compliment to his German, this made it even more amazing and comical, like the Santa Claus hood jammed on the mop of his already greying Afro hair.

It was at this point that Frau Schleting, who had apparently only just realized he was there, came over. That was the start of the disaster. 'My Spanish Santa Claus! Oh, *que viva España!*' she shouted gaily. From somewhere high above him – she was an uncommonly tall woman – she offered him her slender, bejewelled hand, gripping him vigorously in the handshake, but then letting herself fall on to the sofa so suddenly that for a moment he was scared she might crash on top of him. She swept back her hair and, nibbling at the rim of her glass, stared at him with passionate eyes.

He had no idea how to respond, beyond folding his white-gloved hands over his stomach that bulged in the tight red jacket, and shooting a worried look in the direction of Herr Schleting. The latter, doubtless out of a sense of propriety, preferred to pretend he hadn't seen a thing, the only sign of any impatience on his part being the way he drummed the heel of his patent leather shoe on the thick-piled carpet.

Then, with what was an apparently careless gesture, Frau Schleting had started to run a fingernail up and down his trouser leg, mirroring the movement with her lips round the rim of the glass. He glanced again at Herr Schleting, who this time pursed his lips and shook his head in annoyance.

He had stood up to say goodbye, get his money and leave, but was forcibly held back. She clawed at his arm and made him sit down again, ensnaring him with burning glances. This time, when he collapsed disheartened on to the sofa, there was no need to look over imploringly at Herr Schleting. He at last had begun to rebuke his wife, in his quiet, steely voice: she was not behaving as she should, it was unworthy of her to give a false impression to foreigners like that – stressing the word *foreigners* to emphasize how unthinkable her conduct was; even though the festivities excused a certain amount of goodwill, he begged her to regain her composure. All this accompanied by a tiny stretched smile, yet another demonstration of his unfailing politeness.

It had started to snow. The snow fell silently past the windows; as always, it filled him with wonder and delight, although this didn't in any way lessen his embarrassment at the mess he was in. He was the only one who noticed the snow. Suddenly, Frau Schleting proposed a toast to Christmas and to Spain. Without waiting for her husband to agree, she filled their glasses, the champagne overflowing on to table and carpet.

Bound by the strictures of his courtesy, Herr Schleting stood up and drank. He too was forced to toast, swallowing the champagne as quickly as he had the beer. This merely meant that she filled his glass again, splashing wine down the front of his costume; and each time he emptied it, anxious to be off, she refilled it, serving herself at the same time.

Herr Schleting, who some time before had placed his own glass well out of reach, now slapped his knees as he made to rise. He wished to thank Mister . . . who must have other appointments to keep, other homes to visit that night, and so it must be time to say farewell. At this Herr Schleting rose to his feet and with the same elegant, unruffled gesture as he had ushered him in, made to show him the door.

How many glasses of Mumm had Frau Schleting plied him with? He hadn't the faintest idea. He had already tossed aside his red hood, so that now it was his bushy Afro hair that Frau Schleting was ogling, chattering all the time about Spain. He lounged back on the sofa, no longer protesting as she continued to fill his glass, guffawing as he tried to explain that he had nothing to do with Spain, and uninvited holding forth about Venezuela – the plains, *Alma Llanera*, the mountains, the people from his home town Maracaibo, the forest of oil derricks on the lake, the heat, and how you could fry an egg at noon on the pavement in Maracaibo. He was even telling jokes about dictators and Pérez Jiménez, but these didn't even raise the flicker of a smile on Herr Schleting's face.

It was still snowing outside, but by now he hated the idea of this dirty, freezing snow, the slippery surface of the salted pavements, the stale smell of soot in the U-Bahn entrance at Viktorie-Louise-Platz, the dismal lights in the tunnels and the muffled roar of the trains, hated the thought of the eternal smirking giants in their vigil on the walls this Christmas midnight. 'Here's to you,' he had called out, drinking now in his best carefree manner, spreadeagled on the sofa. He unbuttoned the Santa Claus jacket to feel for a Krone, and his red and grey checked lumberjack shirt spilled out. He asked Herr Schleting for a light.

Never for a second had Herr Schleting appeared taken aback by his impertinence. He merely straightened his bow tie and paced up and down, his arms still folded across his chest. Frau Schleting was stretched out on the sofa, and lay there toying with her empty glass. She had slipped off her shoes, and was tickling him with her toes. Suddenly though, she stirred, leapt up and asked him if he knew how to dance 'Que Viva España!'

To which he had replied laughing that he knew nothing about *pasodobles*, that was for fairies: no, he would teach her to dance *joropos*, *cumbias*, *guarachas*, *mambos*. She would have none of that – what she wanted was to dance 'Que Viva España' with her Spanish Santa Claus.

Sometime about then Herr Schleting had slipped into the dining room. From there, as he used his lighter to light the candles, he reminded his wife that their traditional Christmas dinner was waiting on the table. He said this in the same even tone, as though there were only the two of them present and nothing untoward had happened. Her only answer was to repeat that she wanted to dance 'Que Viva España' with her Spanish Santa Claus. She staggered over to a pile of records to look for it. He was snorting with laughter – no, she'd got it all wrong, he wasn't Spanish, where on earth had she got that idea? Herr Schleting, as his wife began to shout *Olé! Olé!* warned in the same soft-spoken cool voice that nobody was going to play 'Que Viva España!' nobody was going to dance 'Que Viva España!'

'Que Viva España! burst from the stereo. It was when she swayed over to him, snapping her fingers to the rhythm like a flamenco dancer, that he had realized the disaster was inevitable.

Inevitable when, in spite of being perfectly aware that Herr Schleting had suddenly disappeared from the dining room, he was fool enough to start dancing with her, and let her pull him close and breathe her yeasty breath into his false beard – *uno, dos, uno, dos, olé!* – while she stroked the back of his neck with a bony, bejewelled hand. Even more inevitable when she tried to pull off his beard to kiss him properly, still beating out the *pasodoble* rhythm and frogmarching him in between the furniture.

All at once the lights went out, and the room was lit solely by the scarlet and emerald decorations of the giant Christmas tree. Not only did Frau Schleting fail to sense the danger, but the darkness seemed to excite her still further. She shouted again at the top of her voice: *que viva España!* locking him in her embrace. The explosions drowned her shout, and fragments of the huge gilt-framed mirror shattered on to the side tables and armchairs. Herr Schleting was standing in a cloud of gunsmoke, calmly cradling a double-barrelled shotgun. He caught a glimpse of the green hunter's cap with its countless badges. Frau Schleting, blissfully unaware of the explosions, went on dancing crazily, all alone. He himself was frantically scrabbling on all fours to find his red hood and the false beard – which Frau Schleting had eventually succeeded in pulling off – because he had to return all the items of the costume. As he crawled over to the door two more loud bangs rang out, followed by another two as he fled headlong down the stairs.

Now, back in the damp loneliness of his room in Manitus-strasse he is sitting on the bed smoking his very last Krone. The red flashes from the patrol cars down in the yard spiral up towards his window, lending the frosty window-panes an oven-like glow. He can hear the hollow sound of the policemen's footsteps as they climb to arrest him for being a foreigner who has disturbed the peace of a German home. The Santa Claus costume is draped over the same armchair in which he has sat for so many years poring over engineering textbooks without ever understanding a thing. Filled with the bitterness and frustration he'll take back with him to Maracaibo, he knows in an instant that he'll be dubbed, with pitying sarcasm: *the German*. For ever.

Translated by Nick Caistor

Chicken for Three

FERNANDO SILVA

The sergeant shifted in his chair and gave the Indian a long hard look.

'So you're the one who steals Father Hilario's chickens, are you?' he said.

The Indian looked at the ground. Flinging back his chair, the sergeant leapt to his feet.

'This Indian doesn't know it's a sin to steal from the father,' he said to another man standing next to him, a sheaf of papers in his hand. The man chortled.

'It's no laughing matter,' the sergeant said, a serious expression on his face. 'You'll see,' he said, wagging a finger at the Indian: 'I'm going to lock you up and make you pay for every one of those chickens you stole from the father.'

The Indian's eyes darted up at the sergeant. He protested, frowning: 'I never ate them chickens.'

'Well, who did then?' the sergeant pressed him.

'A fox, maybe . . .' the Indian said.

This time it was the sergeant's turn to laugh. 'Ha ha, so it was a fox, was it? The only fox around here is you. Yeah, a smart black-haired fox, aren't you just?'

'But . . . it's true,' the Indian spluttered.

'Don't you try to make a fool of me. There were witnesses who saw you carrying off the chickens.'

'Those weren't the father's birds.'

'Whose were they then?'

'Well . . . they weren't chickens, anyway. They were nothing but a bunch of feathers.'

'What feathers?'

'I was walking down on the other side, you see . . . and I saw all these feathers . . . "Aha," I said to myself. "Perhaps I can use them for a pillow." So I picked them up, and it was just then that the priest – he must have been out searching for his chickens – caught sight of me and shouted: "Caught you red-handed, Ramón! You're stealing my chickens"! "What chickens?" I asked him. "Can't you see these are only a bunch of feathers?" "That's as may be," the priest told me, "but they're my chickens' feathers" . . . that's how it was, Sergeant, I swear.'

The sergeant walked to the door. Outside, it was pouring with rain. 'This Indian's no fool,' he thought to himself.

Father Hilario was trimming his paraffin lamp.

'Good afternoon, Father,' the sergeant greeted him.

'Good afternoon, my son.'

'I've caught that Indian Ramón, the chicken-thief.'

'You have to punish him, Sergeant. It's your duty. That's how they all start. Give them a chicken and they take a horse. It's the same with sin . . . at first, it's a mere trifle, but then it gets worse and worse.'

'Father,' the sergeant interrupted him, 'are you sure the Indian stole your chicken?'

'What's that? Am I sure? Didn't I see him with my own two eyes? What on earth do you mean?'

'Ramón claims it wasn't a chicken he was carrying.'

'Not a chicken? What was it then?'

'I'm not sure . . . but what exactly did you see?'

'My chicken . . . that's what I saw!'

'All right, whatever you say . . . but I've brought the Indian along anyway, so you can have it out face to face.'

The Indian came in, hat in hand. The sergeant, a vague smile on his face, leaned back on a table propped against the wall. The father laid aside his lamp.

'So now you deny you took the chickens?' the father said.

'I'm not denying anything,' the Indian muttered.

'There you are then, Sergeant,' the father exclaimed.

'What I told the sergeant . . .' the Indian went on, 'is that you never saw me with your chicken.'

'What? I didn't see you? Didn't I shout to you: "Hey Ramón, leave that chicken alone?" And didn't you run off?'

'Yes, I ran off all right, but running away doesn't mean I stole your chicken. There's no law against running, is there?'

'Oh, no,' the priest replied,' you stole my chicken and no mistake.'

'No, Father . . . it was only feathers . . .'

'Feathers! You thief! And you're still trying to twist everything. May God punish you for stealing from a poor priest . . .!'

The sergeant put on his cap, clapped the Indian on the shoulder, and barked: 'Let's go.'

The priest stared at the two men.

'He'll have to pay for the chicken,' he insisted.

The sergeant went out with the Indian.

'You see,' he said. 'That priest is right. You stole his chicken, and now you'll have to pay for it.'

The Indian stopped in his tracks and stared at the sergeant.

'That was no chicken,' he said.

'What was it then?' asked the sergeant.

'No more than a spider,' the Indian replied. 'It was nothing but a bundle of feathers. I had to spend good money fattening it up . . . it was all skin and bone. That's why I said it was no chicken . . . it was a bunch of feathers! But you should see it now, Sergeant, it's lovely and plump.'

The sergeant gazed down at him.

'Go and bring it for the father then. Hand it back to him.'

'All right,' the Indian replied, 'but didn't you say that as tomorrow's a holiday you'd be coming to my place to eat?'

'Oh, it's tomorrow, is it?' the sergeant said thoughtfully, coming to a halt.

'Yes, tomorrow,' the Indian said, smiling as he shuffled away.

The sergeant turned on his heel and, with the rain still pouring down, hurried back to his office.

Translated by Nick Caistor

PARAGUAY

Under Orders

HELIO VERA

Of course I recognize the place. You came to the right man for that. Regalado Montiel, the best hunter in Piripucú, and the best known. A highly paid guide what's more, not the kind you fob off with five *reales* or a few provisions. A veteran of the 1870 war, from Corrientes on. A sergeant-major in the army of Marshal Francisco Solano López, part of his escort. He trusted me completely and I stuck closer to him than his own shadow.

This is the place all right. Just as I left it thirty years ago. Behind the reedbed, just a couple of miles along a good track and down a slope. Everything's just as it was then. The same putrid smell of stagnant water on every gust of wind. The same swarms of butterflies and the murky yellow light that the trees let through, and the undergrowth so thick you need a machete to hack your way through.

These are the marks that we left then, in 1870, when we came here under orders from Karaí Guasú López, as we called the marshal, to hide the treasures of the fatherland, to stop them falling into the hands of the Brazilians or being shared out amongst those turncoats who joined the Paraguayan Legion. I can see the old scars on the bark. They still point, like an arrow, towards the rosewood tree growing up against the side of the bank, tall as a cathedral.

The marks are higher up now, of course, and a bit blackened. Now they're nearly above my head. Much higher than when we made them with our machetes, myself and Josías and the Indians who were with us then. You see, sir, trees grow just like people do. Each of them looking for a bit of space higher up than the others, to get a breath of air out in the warm sun.

It was me who found the place. The stream widens here and forms a pool of deep, black water. You can't get a good idea of its size, not now it's covered with all those water-lilies that the floodwaters have swept downstream from who knows how many miles away. The strong current will carry them off again sometime, the water will subside and leave the earth clean and fresh.

You'd never think there was all that gold down there, all mixed up with the mud on the bottom of the pool. Gleaming amid the rotten wood of the boxes. They've probably still got the emblem of the Republic stamped on them, the morning star.

All that wealth just sleeping there. Poisoning the water, dazzling the fishes. Old gold for melting down. Silver rosaries with eleven mysteries. Precious stones. Hooped earrings. Intricately woven rings. Gold coins. English sovereigns. Filigree work by jewellers from Luque. Wrought silver from the churches.

Now you can hardly see the great heavy chain wound round the rosewood tree. The links have cut so deep into its bark they're almost part of its wood now, bathed in its sap. Then it snakes down to the pool and gets lost amongst the ferns. It plunges into the still water, down until it curls around each of the sealed crates. Like a long, hungry serpent of iron. We had a hell of a job bringing the chain this far. It was so heavy we could barely lift it on to the cart.

It was Karaí Guasú López himself who gave me the order. It was the night we reached the shores of the Kapiibary lagoon, at the source of the Ypané Guasú. We'd crossed the mountains twice and were drifting aimlessly across the countryside of Jerez. The soldiers were just skin and bone, exhausted by hunger. Five thousand of us had begun the retreat north but by then there were no more than five hundred left. The others got left behind, for good.

We were looking for the approach to the ford across the Chirigüelo river that would lead us to Cerro Corá. The marshal thought we would be safe there, where the mountain chain forms a sort of stone basin, hidden in an inaccessible place, easy to defend. There were only a few more miles to go. We were on the last stretch.

There were no white men in those desolate areas. Just a few marauding Indians around the hills of Sarambí and

Guasú. Sometimes, far off, we caught sight of their campfires and heard their singing. According to them the centre of the earth is in Ybypyté, near by in the mountains.

The rain had pelted down those last few days. We all felt weak and battered. That night, people lay down in the mud as best they could or made shelters for themselves in the branches of trees. Only the ragged sentries moved about the camp, clutching their rifles, their eyes watchful.

We'd just finished our supper, some bits of leather strapping that we'd boiled in water to make edible. Just a trick to fool our empty stomachs. The marshal sent for me. They hadn't unloaded the carts carrying the treasure yet. These stood near at hand under heavy guard. By lamplight we made an inventory of their contents, with Vice President Sánchez acting as scribe.

And they handed it all over to me, in exchange for a receipt, with orders to put it in some safe, secret place. I remember the date – 29 January 1870 – and Sánchez's whispering voice as he read out the contents of the load.

When he'd finished reading, Karaí Guasú López ordered the others to withdraw. We were alone, just the two of us. He gave me detailed instructions on what I should do. I had to go over the details three times before he was satisfied I'd understood everything.

He put his hand on my shoulder and looked at me long and hard. He was silent, thoughtful, I think the idea went through his head that I might betray him too. Like so many others who had gone off on the slightest pretext. In the end his own brothers, his brothers-in-law and even his mother plotted to poison him.

It was a tremendous responsibility he was giving me. Only ten days before Major Félix García, a brave and loyal soldier, had deserted. He'd been entrusted with a carriage-load of jewellery and precious stones belonging to the marshal's mother and sisters and had just gone off with it. Greed is a powerful thing, sir, that can trouble the souls of the most moderate men.

Karaí Guasú López himself gave me the password I needed to get through the checkpoints. He hung a scapular bearing the image of the Holy Virgin round my neck, and ordered me to start off at once. Hardly anyone noticed the carts leaving the camp. The guard, still half asleep, let me through, scarcely bothering to listen to the password he demanded from me.

They gave me five Indians for the oxen and as escort. They were the best-looking and strongest of what was left of the battalion of scouts. Each of them was armed with a sabre, a lance and a Turner rifle. We carried provisions, just the minimum to survive. Almost nothing really. A little manioc flour and a few strips of dried meat. But there was no need to worry. The Indians know how to fend for themselves. They eat snakes, toads and mice with as much gusto as if they were dining out at the Club Nacional. Even in the thickest undergrowth they can spot an armadillo's burrow, a wasps' nest oozing honey or a tapir's lair. They'll even eat those white grubs that collect in rotten tree trunks if they have to. Nothing seems to disgust them. I've seen them in Ygatimí eating the crackling from a roast dog and licking their fingers with relish.

As adjutant I had Captain Josías Maldonado. We'd been together so long I loved him like a brother. He was very much weakened by malaria and a suppurating wound he'd had since Ita Ybaté. And the goitre on his neck was getting bigger and uglier all the time. But that was hardly surprising. None of us wandering through that godforsaken place was exactly in good shape.

We left in the middle of a storm. The ground shuddered with each roll of thunder. Every now and then, just by chance, we glimpsed each other's face lit by a flash of lightning. Shortly after dawn the sky cleared a little and there before us were the Seven Sisters and the Southern Cross to give us our bearings. The Indians were singing softly to themselves about something or other.

Once we were a good way off from the camp we got talking, Josías and me. We knew we were in for a long haul, and talked and talked, going over events we'd lived through. Our words took on the rhythm of our horses' short steps, at the head of our caravan.

We travelled many miles from the camp to this place. We plunged into the currents of streams, walked through swamps, over rocks. We zigzagged like crazy men. Just to be sure no one was following us.

There were plenty of people who would have given anything to pick up our trail. With a good Indian guide there's no prey you can't run to ground. For just a few coins and a bottle of rum they could have been persuaded to come after us and be right on our heels.

You don't know these Indian scouts. Eyes like a hawk and a sense of smell as keen as a hunting dog's. They don't miss a thing when they're tracking, tiny details no white man would ever spot. The branch of a tree at an odd angle to the wind. The way a twig's been broken underfoot. The smell and warmth of a pile of excrement. The ashes of a fire. With help like that we could have been in real trouble. But, luckily for us, no one came.

We wandered on through this wilderness with no clear idea of where we were heading to carry out our orders. But we went on looking, feeling our way blindly. I marked our route on a small map. Several times the carts got stuck in the bog and we had to use brute force to drag them out. There's no one like the Indians for that. Just as well they were in better physical shape than the rest of the soldiers. All because they were quite happy to eat grubs and suchlike that no one else would touch.

That last night as it grew dark we left the reedbeds and emerged on to dry land. Behind the ridge was the perfect place. I lay down to rest right there and prayed to the Virgin Mary, clutching the scapular to me.

We had to slaughter one of the lead oxen that had gone lame on us just as we arrived. It was the first time in weeks that we'd eaten real meat. Otherwise we'd survived on palm sprouts, bitter oranges, coconuts and papaya.

We spent the rest of the night breaking up the carts. We had to get rid of the last traces of evidence that we'd been here. We tied the chain round this tree. Then we tied the other end to each of the boxes and threw them into the pool, along with what was left of the carts. When at last we could rest it was getting light. Our limbs shook as if we had St Vitus's dance.

You're probably wondering why Karaí Guasú López chose

me, Regalado Montiel, for this mission. Well, I was brought up by the López family from when I was a little boy. Don Carlos's brother, Don Francisco de Paula López found me in a timberyard in Yuty. My mother had died of the fever when I was only a year old and not even weaned. The evil eye got my father and I can scarcely remember his face. Just the warmth of his poncho when he rocked me to sleep in winter.

I settled in the town of Trinidad as a servant in Don Carlos's house. It was a nice, safe job with no worries or hardships. Every morning before sunrise, when the morning star was still bright, I made him his *maté*. I used to add herbs to the kettle boiling on the hearth, herbs to help him urinate better and to break up kidney stones: sumach, soapberry, burdock, myrtle, sorrel. Then Don Carlos would give me his blessing and all kinds of sound advice, tips on how to get on in life. Once he gave me a Bolivian coin.

Don Francisco de Paula died in Caazapá. They buried him beneath a marble tombstone, together with his sword of gold. I wept inconsolably because I owed him so much. Don Carlos used to say that the worst sin you can commit is ingratitude. And that the worst place in hell is reserved for traitors and people who go back on their word. Like that relative of his, Don Manuel Pedro de la Peña, who ate at his table and then cursed his government when he got to Buenos Aires.

When Don Carlos died I was left in the charge of his son, Francisco Solano López. He enlisted me in the army. You should have seen me, sir, with my grenadier's boots and my Acâ Verá helmet. The red jacket, the frogging, the shining buttons, the chin strap, and at my side the gold-tasselled sabre made for cutting and thrusting.

It was my job to watch over Karaí Guasú López while he slept and to guard him discreetly at every moment. I would follow a short distance behind him, trying not to be noticed, but alert to what might come from any direction. If necessary I was to block any hostile attack with my own body. Blending in with the scrub or a still shadow behind a pillar, I was always ready. Even when he went on his forays after women outside the town.

Have a bit more of this venison, sir. It's as tender and tasty as a woman's backside. You can see where I get my reputation as the best hunter in these parts. I've got the best aim of anyone around here. I killed the animal with one shot, right in the head. He just gave a leap and fell down dead.

When the war began, from Cerro León onwards, the marshal put me in the military training school. Can't you just see it, sir, the cream of the soldiery, the army of the fatherland. The best soldiers came from there, the battalions that Lakú Estigarribia surrendered in Uruguayana without putting up so much as a struggle. He didn't even have the gumption to try an attack. He was so conceited, puffed up like a prize cockerel, but he turned out to be a coward, who backed down at the first sign of trouble.

I was in Corrientes with General Robles's column. We evacuated the city after the Brazilian ironclads sank our best boats in Riachuelo. Robles was tried for incompetence and shot.

Then came the campaign in the south. We had to march waist deep through reedbeds, through low-lying areas full of snakes, centipedes and spiders as big as my fist. I fought on Purutué island, in Estero Bellaco, in Sauce. I never once turned my back on the Brazilians.

In Tuyutí the marshal intended finishing off the enemy at one stroke, but instead we lost almost all our men. I managed to escape, thank God, galloping off on a bay that snorted with fear, maddened by the smoke and the noise. With the Olabarrieta cavalry we circled the whole of the allied camp looking for General Barrios's battalions. But Barrios was nowhere to be found and he never arrived. It was a complete disaster.

If you ask me, that Barrios was up to something, it became common knowledge he was plotting against Karaí López. When he was finally charged he cut his throat with a razor but they found him in time and after that he had a little high voice, like the shrill scratchy music of *gualambáu*. Afterwards he made out he was mad, pretending to be terrified of everything, even an ant passing by. That didn't stop us shooting him.

That night in Tuyutí there was music in our camp. The Para'í band played 'La Palomita' with a kind of desperation, almost fury. To show the enemy that they hadn't broken us and we were still in good spirits. There were so many dead that the allies couldn't bury them all. They piled them up like so much firewood and set light to them. The bodies of our men took days to burn up completely. They'd got so thin, you see, there was no fat on them. They were just scrawny, hard, leathery flesh, like the black dried meat that's left over in January.

No one had ever seen anything like it, sir, so much courage just squandered. And that wasn't the worst of it. The disease and poverty in the camp killed as many of our men as the allies had. But we had to put up with it all and swallow our pride so as not to give them too cheap a victory.

Some just didn't have the guts for it and were easily disheartened. The seed of betrayal was planted and grew up around the campfires and the stacked rifles. Like the *ura*, the temptation of Judas laid its eggs beneath the skin of many honourable and trustworthy men.

Things looked up for us at Curupayty but the defeats that followed put paid to our hopes of victory. Even so we remained at our posts at the side of our leader, Karaí Guasú. Without him we would have felt lost, not knowing where to turn, like madmen adrift in a dark night.

Traitors were springing up everywhere like weeds after rain, and we had to get rid of them. In San Fernando on the Tebicuary, to rid ourselves once and for all of that scum, I carried out orders that still trouble my conscience. In Lomas Valentinas, just before the battle, we shot scores of elegant, high-class people, amongst them Colonel Paulino Alén. He'd been my commanding officer in the training school. A good man, the colonel, who'd proved his worth in battle. There weren't many braver than him in combat. He was witty too and carried himself well, like an English gentleman. He was agile as a cat when he danced the *cielito* and one glance from his blue eyes sent the women wild.

Poor Alén. The Humaitá affair wasn't his fault but we couldn't just let it pass. The marshal held him responsible for several blunders. Alén felt overwhelmed by the failure and shot himself in the head, though he didn't die. The rout at Uruguayana broke him, and his wound left him confused, disoriented.

He was lucky that we shot him really, because he'd never

have been able to walk again. We bundled him up inside a leather bag and I opened a few holes in it so that he could relieve himself. We hung him up like that in a tree and there he stayed, more or less forgotten. Sometimes inside the bag he laughed out loud like a madman. He seemed deranged. He was just skin and bone when we came for him. The bag was strangely still when he was brought before the firing squad. It only quivered slightly when the bullets struck. I still don't know if it was the impact of the bullets that made him shudder or just a last tremor of the flesh before he gave up the ghost.

Don José Berges, Minister for Foreign Affairs, died with him. He was a charming man, honest and very well read. I owed him several favours. He was always good to me and I had nothing against him. But I was the one who seized him and clamped the irons on his legs. He just looked at me and said nothing. He knew as well as I did that orders were orders. We shot him together with Alén, Bishop Palacios, General Vicente Barrios, the marshal's brother-in-law, and several others. The court martial had called for them to be hanged, but General Resquín wouldn't agree to it. They were shot, sitting down, from behind.

Minutes later the battle started. The shots from the firing squad mingled with the first shots from the enemy. Those seven days of fighting finished us. It's a miracle I survived. When there wasn't a man left standing, the marshal left, trotting off on his horse towards Potrero Mármol. He sat very upright on his mount, his gaze far off, as if he were dreaming. The only movement he made was now and again to flick his gold-handled whip. He seemed absent, already somewhere else.

The shells fell and exploded harmlessly at our feet. Karaí López didn't even blink, just kept his eyes fixed on the road. There couldn't have been many more than a hundred troops following him, within sight of the enemy who merely fired off a few shots at us. That was the end of our last army. What came later, even Cerro Corá, didn't seem like war any more, just misfortune.

I was with Colonel Hermosa in Caaguy Yurú to cover the retreat to the north. The Brazilians were on us like a swarm of wasps and we had to give them a fight. But it was futile. Those who didn't die scattered into the hills. The Brazilians beheaded the field officers and officers they captured. They laid them out in two rows on the ground, each body separated by about a yard from its head. General Victorino Carneiro Monteiro rode his golden bay down this avenue of bones, not even deigning to look to either side.

The journey north was so terrible I still have nightmares about it. The jaguars acquired a taste for white man's flesh. They lay down by the paths, fat and sleepy. All they had to do was wait until some straggler no longer had the strength to go on. High up in the sky the crows made circles, waiting.

They say that when a storm threatens up near the Chirigüelo gorge you can still hear the moans and shouted orders. It's quite commonplace to come across ghosts there, soldiers carrying lances and wearing their loincloths and the leather shako of our army. They're so thin you can count their ribs. I myself saw Colonel Alén again, weighed down by the disgrace at Uruguayana, and Biship Palacios reproaching me with sacrilege for having shot him. Plagues of dead men, bringers of ill omen.

We executed more traitors in Zanja hû, above the Arroyo Guazú. This time to save scarce ammunition we used our lances. As the situation worsened, disloyalty became rife. Ah, but you should have seen Consolación de Barrios's white skin. To avoid looking at her executioners she tossed her head twice so that her long hair fell over her eyes. When the iron pierced her skin, she didn't let out so much as a sigh. Hilario Marcó was put to the lance in that very same spot, the general who only months before had ordered the shooting of General Barrios. Odd the turns life takes, up and down like a carousel horse.

We left more than seven hundred sick and wounded there, unable to move. We couldn't carry them, so the marshal left them to the mercy of the Brazilians. But they took a different route and went another way in their pursuit. The seven hundred died of course, probably of hunger, eaten by worms. Years later some gentlemen who were marking out the frontier with Brazil found their skeletons scattered throughout the camp. The eyeless heads seemed to be looking towards the approach to the gorge, where they were sure the Brazilians would come from. They'd waited in vain.

What else could we do but follow orders? Besides, there weren't only traitors, there were those too who kept their heads and remained loyal. I remember Colonel Bernardino Denis, the oldest commanding officer in our army. He sensed he was dying during the journey to Cerro Corá; and just lay down by the path. He called me over and gave me his sabre and his kepi to present to the marshal. He was quite calm and still had time to ask me to remember him to various friends. Then he opened his eyes very wide as if to see me better and fell back.

What can I say, sir? I was one of those sworn to die with Karaí Guasú López. I had to go on to the bitter end. And I carried that oath in my heart, not just on my lips. But in Cerro Corá I broke my promise.

I wasn't at his side in Aquidabán when the Brazilians killed him. Captain Francisco Argüello and Corporal Chamorro defended the few yards that separated the marshal from his enemies. They had to cut the two of them to pieces to reach him, then they shot him at point-blank range.

Very early that morning some women had come running up from the Tacuaras pass to warn us that the Brazilians were there. The marshal gave me urgent orders to go and look, while he called the men to arms. When I got there with four soldiers, the Brazilians had already captured our sentries. We tried to gallop to a nearby clump of trees but they cut off our path. There was no way we could retreat then and they attacked and cornered us.

We had to fight our way out. I remember the shouting, the gasps, the horses lunging, the sparks from the clashing sabres, a black soldier laughing. I laid about me and I think I wounded an officer because he left the skirmish, only just managing to hold himself upright in his saddle.

I was struck on the head and fell to the ground. I woke many hours later when the sun was rising. They'd tied me to a tree with a very fine rawhide thong that cut into my flesh. Because of the blood on my face I couldn't really see what was going on. I heard cheering, the moans of a wounded soldier, the music of a dance starting up in the camp where graves had recently been dug. A woman was shrieking with laughter, God knows why.

Someone staggered up to me. He shouted at me in Portuguese, then put a glass to my mouth and let me drink. It tasted like champagne, booty from the marshal's cellar. I guessed then that it was all over. I cried in gratitude for the drink but knew that my pact with Karaí Guasú López was stronger than ever. The scapular he had given me in Kapiibary burned against my skin like hot coals.

They took me to Asunción as a prisoner, locked up in a cage, but once there they released me and took no further notice of me. I slept many nights in the corridor of the harbour master's office. When I could, I made my way back to this part of the country. I was hired as paymaster working for a gringo, near the Tacuatí chapel. Then I concentrated on hunting, never straying too far away from here.

Every now and then someone comes and asks me to take them to the place where we left the carts. I don't know how word got around. But I've been ready for a long time to make the trip. I know the route almost by heart, even with my eyes closed.

That's why the Indians died, from the poisoned ox meat. Or rather from the poison I mixed with the salt. The brutes took several hours dying, rolling around in the mud, looking at me with accusing eyes. They muttered things, probably terrible things, in their own language. But what could I do but follow my orders?

I had to kill my adjutant Josías as well, once we'd finished burying the Indians. I put a bullet through his head. I don't think he could have felt a thing. He was kneeling down, praying, and he just fell forward on to the freshly dug earth. I'm sure he'd have understood, that he'd have forgiven me. We were both brought up to carry out orders with no fuss, no questions asked.

When morning came it was raining gently. I noticed Josías's blood flowing down towards the stream, leaving his face clean. The rain washed the ants away and left it with an odd, almost friendly expression. Like when he used to tell jokes in camp. That morning Josías looked the picture of peace and humility.

Around me was the murmur of birds singing. A hare scuttled between my legs. Butterflies gathered around Josías and a rainbow stretched from one side of the stream to the other. Then I knew that all was well and I could rest easy.

It took me a day and a half to get back, bringing the remaining oxen and even what was left of the meat. Karaí López just stared at me and couldn't speak. I'm sure he'd long ago given up hope of seeing me again. He must have thought I was going to run off with the carts and turn myself over to the enemy, just like all the others who had licked his boots before. People with the souls of petty tradesmen like Colonel Lázaro Quevedo, Colonel Carmona and the doctor, Solalinde, who all scurried off like lizards with some story about going to explore the surrounding area.

But you already knew part of this story, sir. That's how you knew where to find me in that bar in Tacuatí and why you offered me all that money to bring you here. It was very kind of you to buy me the rum and *guaviramí* and the new studded saddle you gave me as a sign of good faith.

What I should tell you is that even after Cerro Corá I still felt bound by my orders. That's why the two of us are here alone and why you're pointing a gun at me. Presumably you intend to kill me.

In this hollow scapular I wear round my neck I still keep the poison Karaí Guasú López gave me to kill the Indian escort he assigned me. There was enough left for you. But it's nearly all gone. Anyway I'm getting old now. That's why I'm telling you this story. To give you time to kill me and to have done once and for all with the orders Karaí Guasú gave me thirty years ago. You won't outlive me by much. I used up the poison on the venison you've just eaten. Soon your belly will start to burn and your senses become confused. And I can finally report back to Karaí Guasú that his orders have been carried out.

Translated by Margaret Jull Costa

PERU

Anorexia with Scissors

ALFREDO BRYCE ECHENIQUE

He was never, nor had ever claimed to be, what you might exactly call a man of scruple, and was even less of one when things were going well for him. And things had been going extremely well for him recently, until that damned Scamarone business, which meant he had become a thoroughly unscrupulous man indeed. This idea, this conclusion rather, suddenly seemed distinctly unappealing, so Joaquín Bermejo left off soaping his right arm and began on his left, noting with annoyance yet again that whereas other men came face to face with themselves at night on their pillows, or in the morning when they shaved, he was the exception to the rule in that he could only face up to himself under the shower's noisy jet.

So he cursed Raquelita, because she and her anorexia slept too close by to allow him to confide any secrets to his pillow and because *scrawny, faded, and past it* as she was, the skin and bones of anorexia, Raquelita and her odious, exasperating anorexia were quite capable of wandering unannounced into the bathroom, quite capable of catching him unawares while he was busy shaving some dirty linen in the mirror.

But the moment he shouted out you sick old goat, daughter of a pair of so-and-sos, to think I still have to perform with you when you're nothing but a heap of skin and bone, when his ideas and observations became hopelessly mixed up with the foulest insults, was when the-until-the-day-before Minister of Labour and Public Works, with chauffeur, limousine, bodyguards and policemen guarding his house, suddenly felt himself utterly and abjectly alone, in the buff and all alone, the ex-minister naked and alone and totally different from all other mortals because all other mortals come face to face with themselves on their pillows or in their mirrors whereas me and nobody else but me, nobody I know at any rate, I am forced to use the shower as a pillow or mirror.

Oh, to hell with the lot of them, he said in the end, but then he was thinking of the Scamarone business and his party at the next elections, kaput, so he would never again find himself the Minister of anything or the Right Honourable anything, not a minister, not anything ever again. To hell with the lot of them.

He turned on the hot and cold water to the full and imagined himself returning to his attorney's practice as ex-minister and, with the elections in another two months a complete disaster, he saw himself a second time returning as ex-minister to his attorney's practice but this time even more shaken because of the elections and because there were moments when this Scamarone business well and truly worried him. So he was a lawyer again, one among many, and in a couple of months his party would be kicked so far out of power that he could never have been further. To hell with the lot of them. As if he had never been in power, and to top it all the Scamarone business.

He began to soap his right leg, reflecting that in his three years as minister he hadn't got as big a slice of the cake as he might have. Or had he? Perhaps he had, though if the yellow press had not scared him with those front-page headlines he might have sliced a bit more out of . . . the Scamarone Affair, as the gutter press had taken to calling it. He shifted both hands and the bar of soap over to his left leg. To hell with the lot of them. On and on about the Scamarone affair, would they never get tired of it? When would they find something better? When are they going to leave me in peace? They were capable of going on . . . quite capable of going on and on, and then the next government . . . Joaquín Bermejo let out another 'to hell with the lot of them' and began to rinse himself off with the next government . . .

So it was no go for the trip to Europe with Vicky. No go for meeting her in Mexico, a week in Acapulco, then off round Europe together, with nobody any the wiser. EX-MINISTER BERMEJO FLEES COUNTRY. He could see the headline, could read it in his mind's eye, so it was no go as far as the trip went. Vicky would be furious. Well, he'd buy her something special to calm her down, he'd explain between kisses that the trip was impossible for the moment, try to be patient, Vicky, it's only for a few months until all this blows over, just try to be patient. He would manage to calm her down in the end, but in between the kisses he would have to face those cunning, penetrating eyes of hers, a wicked look from Vicky to her ex-minister, are you so scared of them, Joaquí? The vixen . . .

Raquelita, though, would swallow his explanation, he would hardly need to explain anything, hardly need to invent an excuse for postponing the lengthy, urgent business trip he had talked of. Raquelita would swallow it just as easily as she always swallowed everything, everything except those three wretched peaches of her anorexia. And he wouldn't have to buy her any expensive present, and she didn't call him Joaquí in between kisses, Raquelita calling him Joaquí in between kisses, my God, perish the thought . . .

And then Joaquín Bermejo, slamming off both taps, let himself go and shouted: the goat, the scrofulous old anorexic goat. And burned himself for his pains, shutting off the cold before the hot, damn and blast it. He scalded himself simply because he was no longer a minister, no, not simply because of that, he'd scalded himself as well because that old goat Raquelita had not even the faintest notion of what the gutter press might be, and above all he'd scalded himself because the bag of bones who was his wife, the mother of his three children, the heiress and owner of all they had possessed until he had become a minister, Raquelita, she of the family name, Raquelita, the anorexic, and anyway, if she had known of the existence of the gutter press, what would she have said? Joaquín Bermejo could hear her very words: they're the dregs of society, Joaquín, as he flung back the shower curtain and came face to face with himself as even less of a minister than before, in a bathroom that was no longer the same bathroom as before.

His tie. The children had already left for school and in the dining room, as ever, despite there being no police guard on the door any more, Raquelita (cup of coffee, not a drop of milk, plus her anorexic peach), Raquelita and his first breakfast without a chauffeur from the Ministry waiting outside for him. It was true, someone had already said it to him, only half in jest, you're going to miss power Joaquín, and oh, it was true. For example, for the first time in three years, once he'd finished his toast, orange juice and his coffee, he would get up and leave in a different direction, head for the pantry and ask the butler to open the garage door so he could drive his car out. He rose from the table, couldn't give a damn that Raquelita was still struggling with her peach, he didn't give her the ritual morning kiss, I'll call you if I can't make lunch, he said, struggling into his jacket. Joaquín, Raquelita suddenly said. He halted, turned to look round at her: what is it?

'Now you're no longer a minister, Joaquín. The children would love to see you at lunch-time.'

Joaquín repeated the whole sequence exactly: he put the jacket back on again as he had done, nothing else for it but to do up another button to put an end to the dialogue with Raquelita, still struggling with her peach. She was staring down at her dish, concentrating on her peach. How delicately she ate it, how delicately she always spoke, Raquelita, the old . . . the old nothing.

'I'll be back in time for lunch with the children. You have my word as a minister, Raquelita.'

The car. Now you're no longer a minister, Joaquín. The children would love to see you at lunch-time. Raquelita had won him over completely. How on earth had she managed it? To begin with, Joaquín reasoned, as he eased the car towards the centre of Lima, if there's anybody in the world who couldn't give a damn whether I'm a minister or not, that person is Raquelita. Of course, her father has been a minister five times, half her family has been a minister five times, and presidents, viceroys and even founders of the city of Lima five times, if such a thing were possible. And secondly, or rather first and foremost from Raquelita's point of view, because she loves me for what I am. Joaquín recalled the scene, despite himself that whole night in the summer garden flashed through his mind, when he had said what he had to say about wanting to marry her.

He'd brought along his brand-new lawyer's diploma.

'Do you love me as I am, Raquelita?'

'Much better than that, Joaquín. I love you for what you are.'

Red light. EX-MINISTER FLEES HIS HOME. EX-MINISTER ABAN-
DONS WIFE AND CHILDREN. SUSPECT IN SCAMARONE AFFAIR
FLEES WITH LOVER. Big trouble. Big trouble brewing if the
next government chose to really investigate. He, no less,
made the scapegoat, the butt for all the jokes and slanders of
the gutter press. Ex-minister Bermejo up to his neck in it . . .
What could his four partners in the law firm be thinking?

Green light, with Raquelita saying they're the dregs of
society, explaining to the children that the people in those
kinds of newspapers and magazines, the people in the new
government, well, really, they were no more than the dregs
of society. Why hadn't he given Raquelita her kiss before he
left? Why hadn't he given her her breakfast kiss? Joaquín
Bermejo's mind filled with quick-fire questions and answers.
He had always cared for her enormously, he always would,
Vicky was bound to leave him in the lurch one of these
days, up to his neck in the Scamarone Affair. Raquelita
would never do anything so indelicate, would never walk
out on him for anything to do with the dregs of society.
And the children, Raquelita, how shall we explain it to the
children? Red light. The children, Joaquín, know perfectly
well these are all things that concern only the dregs of
society.

Green light. Thanks to Raquelita nothing but nothing
would happen, so he could go on always telling the children
that everything they had in life they owed to their father:
take a tip from me, boys, all it takes is a steady hand, a
steady hand and grey matter, that's all, grey matter and a
good, steady hand, take a tip from your old father.

He reached his practice feeling an urgent need to tell his
children all his success had been thanks to his steady hand
and grey matter, lots of grey matter, even steadier hand,
boys. Incredible: he had hardly noticed, but he'd gone into
his own office with the merest nod to the secretaries,
scarcely a word to the clerks, all that remained of the ex-
minister was the gutter press and a whiff of the Scamarone
Affair. The very first thing he did was to call home, send
Raquelita a kiss by phone, and reassure her that yes, he
would be there in time for lunch with them, with you too,
Raquelita. He ended by asking whether she had managed to

finish her breakfast peach. Yes, those were his very words: your breakfast peach, not your anorexic breakfast peach. And he hadn't even felt like strangling her when she confessed she hadn't. Incredible.

Yes, incredible, and slightly grotesque too, even now, but still he had to answer because his secretary was telling him that Miss Vicky, the one with the accent, was on the telephone for him.

'Joaquín, have you seen *La Verdad*?'

'How often do I have to tell you I never read those rags, Vicky?'

'But your little sweet-pie here reads them from cover to cover, Joaquí.'

'I'll call you around half-eight, Vicky. The President has asked to see me at seven. I'll call you tonight as soon as I leave the presidential palace.'

He'd tell her the meeting with the President had lasted until all hours when she called again the next morning. Because today he wanted something different, what he really needed today was to feel that the evening was like the one in the garden, the same night of that garden and that summer, to feel immersed all the evening in that oh-so-far-off night, that never to be repeated garden . . .

'Do you love me as I am, Raquelita?'

'Better than that, Joaquín. I love you for what you are.'

He asked for calls from the presidential palace only to be put through: calls from the presidential palace and from my wife, he added just in time, because they were already on to him, because nobody could stop them now, because what minister had ever been known not to rob, but it was only he who had to face the Scamarone Affair. Otherwise, why had the President called him to the palace? So now they were out there gunning for him, and the flash of their cameras was as violent as the need he felt to confess his most heinous crime. EX-MINISTER ALSO PLANNED TO KILL WIFE! IT ALL HAPPENED IN THE SHOWER! GOLDEN SCISSORS FOIL EX-MINISTER'S ATTEMPT TO MURDER WIFE!

Sobbing, head in his hands but a little calmer, Joaquín Bermejo went over and over the eternal question of which came first, the chicken or the egg. Chronologically, everything was more or less OK. And yet . . . well, marriage of convenience or not, he also was from a good family, and he'd been very much in love when he married, it was simply good fortune that Raquelita, as well as all her other attractions, was part of an excellent, enormously rich family, something he had always wished for, but which had little or nothing to do with the fact that he had married for love, fortunately, like the chicken and the egg. And so Carlos, Germancito, and Dianita were born, the fruits of the love that bound him to Raquelita, fruits of the love binding him to Raquelita like everything in this life, like the chicken and the egg. The fact that his father-in-law had provided his practice with its twelve best clients was just as logical and natural as the chicken and the egg too. The same could be said of the house he inherited from the chicken and the egg, because that was his in-laws' wedding present. OK then, which came first, Raquelita's anorexia or Vicky's tail? Right, Joaquín Bermejo answered his own question, searching deep inside himself for as much sincerity as he could muster, obviously what came first was the chicken or the egg . . .

But it was far simpler to sort out the order of what came next, as he remembered his escapades with Vicky, the constant messages he sent home from the Ministry, Miss Such-and-such, please ask for Mrs Raquelita, Miss So-and-so, please ring my home and tell my wife I have a meeting tonight . . . and there was Vicky on the other line, Vicky demanding more and more each day on the other line, well, the truth is everything had been working out fine ever since he'd reached the Ministry, what better reward could he have asked for than Vicky and her tremendous piece of tail, what's more he had become minister entirely thanks to his own efforts, what more could Raquelita ask for than a man who was the pride of his children, now he could truly say to them it's all down to a steady hand and grey matter, boys, now he really could and no mistake . . . though of course there was no way he could explain the idea of Vicky as compensation for his efforts, they wouldn't understand that, no way they'd understand that he needed that at least in the scales against Raquelita, because your mother, kids, how shall I put it . . . but then again, why was all this explanation necessary, why should he have to be giving an account of himself to his children, he hadn't reached the rank of minister simply to solve the problem of the chicken and the egg. So tonight he'd be with Vicky in his suite at the Crillon, while they could stay home sweet home and look after their dear old mum, with her anorexic peach, the daughter of a . . .

Yes, the worthy daughter of her excellent father and mother, because you had to be not only anorexic but to have been dropped on your head in tender infancy to believe you could defend yourself with a pair of scissors in a city like Lima. Did you ever hear anything so idiotic, Vicky . . .?

'Kiss, kiss, my honey Minister pot?'

First came this crazy anorexia business, one of these days she'll get so thin she'll up and die. Then to top it all, she comes out with this scissor nonsense. So if the anorexia doesn't get her, then someone will bump her off for being so dumb . . .

'Kiss, kiss, sugar lump?'

She really must have been dropped on her head, as well as crazy, if she reckons that in Lima today, they way things are . . . just imagine, Vicky, the house is surrounded with police cars and she thinks she can protect herself with a pair of nail scissors . . .

'Kiss, kiss . . .'

But no, the scissors are made of gold, a thousand carats, and they were the ones the viceroy's wife used to trim her fingernails with, and after her her great-grandmother, then her mother, who passed them on to her, precious family heirloom and all that. And that's just for starters, because it seems that something deep down in her, something in the innermost depths of her being tells her that if anyone in this city rife with the dregs of society should try anything with her . . .

'The what of society, Joaquí?'

'The dregs, sweetheart.'

'What's that when it's at home, angel face?'

'You'll have to ask her that, she's the one who uses the word all the time . . .'

'So the silly old goat reckons she's one of God's chosen, does she?'

'What the silly old goat thinks is none of your business, Vicky.'

'Ooh, my angel's angry, is he? Not leaving me, is he?'

'I've no intention of stirring from here tonight, Vicky. Let's get that at least straight from the start. The rest is all a question of the chicken and the egg, and there's no earthly reason why I have to explain that to my children, to you, or to anyone . . .'

'My, my, we have gone serious, haven't we?'

'No, I promise I won't be, Vicky. On my honour, as a man and as a minister. It's just that she really and truly believes she is invulnerable with that pair of scissors of hers. As though all she believed in were God and her scissors, who allow her to waltz off fancy free all over town, when I've strictly forbidden her to stir outside the house without the chauffeur and a police car to follow them . . . but she's capable of believing it was God's will that thrust the scissors into her hands . . . the family treasure, passed down from hand to hand to hers . . . she's so crazy she'd believe that God . . .'

'Perhaps she'll get herself killed, then we can go off to Acapulco, honeybunch.'

'I'll look after the mother of my children, Vicky, thank you very much. Let's get that straight from the start as well . . .'

The nights of passion with honeybunch went on, week after week, month upon month, nearly three years now, and Vicky grew ever more demanding and the Scamarone Affair had blown up and Raquelita had not been bumped off either by her anorexia or by her stumbling around all over the place with her idiotic trust in God and her pair of scissors. As though God, her anorexia and her golden scissors formed some unassailable trinity. As though, with her faith in God and the knowledge that she was from a good family, from among the best, and the saints knew what more nonsense of the sort . . . incredible . . . the old goat couldn't have been any crazier . . . as though thanks to her pretty face, her three peaches per day, and a pair of scissors handed down from a founder of the city of Lima, no less – that was a piece of news she'd sprung on him one afternoon, the anorexic old goat, as though all this somehow had made of her the mortal enemy, the scourge of all the dregs of society.

The scourge of the dregs, Joaquín Bermejo muttered to himself as he turned the hot and cold water taps full on. Though he was locked in the bathroom, protected still further by the shower curtain, he still needed the sound of the shower water to be louder than ever in order to feel safe enough to indulge himself in all the irrepressible extraordinary thoughts that kept springing to his mind. The scourge of the dregs he smiled happily to himself, as though he had suddenly found the definitive answer to the oldest, most intractable problem of his life. Could he possibly tell Vicky what he was thinking? Tell her that instead of a romantic interlude in Mexico and Europe they could be spending the rest of their lives together, yes, wedding bells, Vicky, yes? He hadn't the faintest idea, but chuckled under the shower, singing while Raquelita, one hundred per cent proof Raquelita was walking calm as a cucumber down a dark Lima street, a street unknown to him except for the fact it contained Raquelita's death on the corner. There, on that very corner, he could see it in his mind's eye, Raquelita pulling her scissors out of her bag while a huge, cool, Negro thug, properly paid and prepared, flashing through his mind's eye clearly and quickly, as quickly and clearly as the quick efficiency of the huge black man disappearing into the night, every inch a professional . . . it was simply a matter of thinking it all through down to the minutest detail . . . there'd be no problem hiring someone like that, Lima was rife with black thugs like that, just as it was rife with ministers like him . . .

Those were the happiest showers of Joaquín Bermejo's life, and he often laughed to himself at that thought that if he had been someone who only took a shower once a week, by now he would be spending the whole day under the shower. He pulled the curtain, turned both taps full on, now what shall I sing while I go over every last minute detail. There was no time to lose: he might be forced to resign from the Ministry over the Scamarone Affair, forced to give up Vicky, who was demanding more every day, and he wanted to give her all he had all he could because he fucking well wanted to, that's why dammit: so Raquelita was a corpse in a pool of blood and even the pair of golden scissors had vanished, that motherfuckin' Negro had even made off with the scissors.

Joaquín Bermejo could not think why he never remembered to tell Vicky of his plans. Nor could he think why they all disappeared into thin air the moment he switched off the shower taps. Could it have something to do with the pillow and the mirror? Disgusted, he was forced to admit yet again that a man comes face to face with himself at night on his pillow or in the morning when he is shaving in his mirror, but he was an exception to the rule because he could only truly face up to himself when he was under the shower's hissing stream.

So it was that one morning, beneath the jet of the shower, Joaquín Bermejo decided to have done with half measures and started to switch off all the hot water while he told Vicky that a huge Negro had laid Raquelita out cold with a single slash of his knife, and now all of us can rest in peace. The news knocked Vicky cold too, but he refused to turn the hot tap on again because for a few weeks at least this is how we'll have to behave, or I at least will have to behave, the coolest head I can manage. Joaquín Bermejo did not flinch from the cold water as he explained to Vicky that she, on the other hand, would have to vanish into thin air until he phoned her again. That will be when everything has settled down again, Vicky, he told her as he switched off the cold water and turned on the hot until he almost scalded himself so that Vicky could vanish in the thin, steam-filled air . . .

The bag of skin and bone sleeping beside me is immortal, Joaquín Bermejo said to himself with a kind of horrified respect as he turned both taps full on the morning he finally realized what it was like to wake up from not one but two dreams at the same time. He could not understand how he had spent day after day toying with the idea of seeing his wife murdered. Immortal old goat, he cursed, having just leapt from bed, after Raquelita, one hundred per cent proof Raquelita in a dream, had calmly put away her scissors while a huge Negro thug fled wounded and panic-stricken . . .

Tie. Breakfast. Quick kiss to bid Raquelita farewell. Joaquín Bermejo began to feel enormously relieved. He hadn't told Vicky a thing, thank God he hadn't said a word to her. That night he only had a couple of drinks with her. He needed to get back home early. He needed to make love to Raquelita, and for her to be aware of his need. So that night Raquelita found herself with a most unusual husband. A Joaquín Bermejo who reminded her of the Joaquín Bermejo of her honeymoon. Afterwards she gazed across at him fast asleep on his pillow and didn't want to wake him when in his restless sleep he began muttering senseless phrases, the only clear thing she could make out, leave me in peace Scamarone. Three times he said that.

At noon there was a call from the presidential palace to inform him that the President would prefer to see him an hour earlier that afternoon, in other words at six, so Joaquín Bermejo calculated that with any luck the meeting would also end an hour earlier than scheduled. There and then he made up his mind to put a stop to this chicken and egg nonsense, he had enough on his plate with Raquelita and Scamarone: full stop amen, why not, everything can be fixed in this arsehole of a country. So instead he'd stop off at the club where, why not, he'd treat himself to a whisky in honour of national reconciliation, why not, then a quick phone call to Vicky Kiss-Kiss. Why not, Joaquín Bermejo? Joaquín Bermejo and Vicky Kiss-Kiss, *por qué no*? Elementary, like two and two make four, Joaquín Bermejo, suck it and see. That's it, right, two and two make four whether it's Lima or Cochinchina. But half an hour later, another call from the presidential palace. The President wished to inform him the meeting would be at five. At five o'clock sharp, the person who telephoned from the palace added, so Joaquín Bermejo's secretary felt obliged to add, at five o'clock sharp, sir.

Joaquín Bermejo reflected that his return to the law practice had hardly been his at all, he said goodbye to the clerks and secretaries in such a way as to say goodbye to them all but to no one in particular, it suddenly occurred to him that not one of his four partners had come out to welcome him back, so he sent word that without fail the next day he would pop in and say a proper hello to each one of them in their offices, then left the plush practice feeling a complete stranger. First the clerks exchanged glances, then the secretaries plucked up courage to look at each other, in the end everybody was staring at everybody else and, like people counting one, two, three, they all burst out together with: Holy cow, the Scamarone Affair! Boy, is he in trouble!

Then Joaquín Bermejo's four partners did appear from their offices. They had been terribly busy in their respective rooms, but now all of a sudden, as though four of them had been born in Fuente Ovejuna, they were of one mind about the Scamarone Affair, as though all four of them had been born during the Trojan Wars as far as the trouble brewing was concerned. Because, just like the Trojan horse, the Scamarone Affair concealed the Finance Bank Affair, and that hid the Assurance Inc. business, and there was even something fishy lurking inside that too, or so it seemed, gentlemen. They were like a chattering clutch of Russian dolls, were Messrs Muñoz Alvarez, Gutiérrez Landa, Mejía Ibañez, and above all Dr Morales Bermejo, whose Bermejo came from his mother's side of the family, but his mother's relation Joaquín Bermejo was no closer than Adam, so any resemblance to reality is purely coincidental, my esteemed colleagues, how about continuing the discussion in the club, we'll have to take some precautionary measures, don't you agree?

But Joaquín Bermejo couldn't take any precautionary measures. He was stuck at home, seated in his luxurious dining room at the opposite end of the table from Raquelita, Carlos and Germán on his left, little Diana on his right, the head of the table as usual, as usual asking the butler what is there for lunch? Except that on this occasion he didn't have the heart to add his usual joke: 'What is there for lunch apart from my wife's anorexic peach?'

He had discovered the horror of being an empty head of the table, he was sitting there experiencing the vast emptiness of being unable to say a steady hand and lots of grey matter, boys. Raquelita and the children were already in the dining room when he arrived, and now there stood the butler with the tray of starters, having just been and gone with the dish containing the peach for the mistress of the house, how hard it was for him to talk of anything with the butler coming and going and his children wolfing down their food to get back to school on time and Raquelita with her crystal serenity, Raquelita one hundred per cent proof. So why, if it had always been like this, did he feel it had never been like this before, or could it be that everyone suspected something already. No, that couldn't be, that really could not be true. In order for it not to be true, in order for there not to be the shadow of a suspicion in the eyes of Raquelita or his children, he spoke to them like a minister:

'The President of the Republic wanted me to see him this afternoon at seven. Then he changed it to six, and in the end he made it five. In view of which, ladies and gentlemen, I propose to arrive there at eight. What do you think of that?'

'At school they reckon the President's nuts,' Carlos announced.

'He doesn't know if he's coming or going,' German added.

'He's a nono,' little Diana summed up.

Joaquín Bermejo smiled at them. He gazed on them as if agreeing with all three, but again after a moment or two felt he was presiding over empty space. There he was, in his usual place, and his children were looking up at him just as they should, but what he had said could not rid him of this feeling he was the empty head faced with an emptiness that stretched for ever before him, and now he would never be able to say to them what he had wanted to say all the three years he had been minister: Take a good look at me, boys, look into my eyes, take a good look and see how your father has become a minister and may one day become President of the Republic as well if he so chooses. And a more valuable President than any of those your mother's family can throw at me, go on, Raquelita, name me one, go on. And Raquelita with her indulgent smile and now at last: do you want to know how I did it? Would you like to know, Carlos? And you, Germán, would you like to know? And of course you want to hear as well, don't you Diana? Well, it was a steady hand and lots of grey matter, steady hand and grey matter, and with the sweat of my brow! With the sweat . . .!

Right there, in the middle of that word sweat, Joaquín Bermejo threw in the sponge. He was worn out, though he hadn't said a single word. He'd broken out into a cold sweat and exhausted himself, and that was all that remained of the sweat of his brow, and it was all the fault of that damned word sweat. That and something worse still, something that was like a commentary on the words which, out of emptiness, he had been unable to utter. Something he discovered when in desperation he looked across at Raquelita.

As with the chicken and the egg, just by her usual manner of eating her peach, nothing more than that, by eating a peach in that manner of hers, Raquelita was telling him: No, Joaquín my love, poor Joaquín, not with the sweat of your brow, not that here among us, Joaquín. A steady hand if you like, yes, although it would be better for you to say effort, consistency, perseverance, and what you call grey matter rather than intelligence, yes, that's fine, you can say that as often as you like, put it first, before everything else in fact. But Joaquín, never ever let me hear you talk again in front of my children of the sweat of your brow or any other words which only the dregs of society employ. Never forget they are my children and that from now on they will be mine more than ever, Joaquín. So please never ever mention things like the sweat of your brow, especially not at table. Not a suggestion of sweat, dearest. In this house, people do not sweat, Joaquín, and especially not in front of the children.

It was then that Joaquín Bermejo discovered his great mistake, the moment he had thought meant one thing but which he now knew meant the exact opposite: he had never hated Raquelita so much as in the garden that fateful summer night when he had asked if she loved him as he was. Wallowing in hatred he realized now he had also hated himself that night. Do you love me as I am, Raquelita? Himself too. Raquelita's real, unbearable reply, now finally: 'I love you for what you are.'

All at once Joaquín Bermejo returned to the crushing splendour of his dining room a changed man, a man who had to make the effort of putting on a face in front of his children, the butler, the enormous sideboard mirror, Raquelita . . . Raquelita, who knew so much more than he ever could, such an enormous amount more, and always had done, so many many things about the chicken and the egg.

'I'm going to talk to my father, Joaquín. You know how he hates the telephone and that he's fishing up at Cerro Azul. So don't worry if I'm late back.'

'Take the chauffeur with you, please.'

'That's impossible, Joaquín. The chauffeur finishes at nine, and that's when I'll just be starting back from Cerro Azul. All I ask of you . . .'

Raquelita broke off in mid-sentence, so the children would not realize something serious was going on. All she added was: 'I'm taking my scissors with me, Joaquín.'

Joaquín Bermejo stared at her from the far end of the table in crushed disbelief, resigned to it all. He looked on silently as she smiled at him from the far rim of the empty world.

'May God go with you, my child,' he said all of a sudden, and the children didn't suspect a thing because their father was always coming out with the weirdest phrases like your anorexic peach or whatever, and anyway Carlos and Germán were rushing to get their things together for afternoon school.

That was the night of his tail between his legs for Joaquín Bermejo. He left the presidential palace close to eight with his tail between his legs, there was going to be a Scamarone Affair and there was going to be a scapegoat. At eleven, tail even further between his legs, he had to take half an hour's tirade from his father-in-law, although he richly deserved to be a scapegoat, there would be no Scamarone Affair. Everything had been fixed with the President and a few other ministers, there would be no Scamarone Affair, but you are a blackguard, Bermejo. If you weren't my daughter's husband and the father of my grandchildren it would have been a different story, Bermejo, I can tell you. Thank your lucky stars, Bermejo. His father-in-law was so irate on the telephone that Bermejo didn't have the nerve to ask him what time Raquelita had left Cerro Azul. He still had his tail between his legs when he decided to call the local police station because his wife had not reappeared and by now it was almost one in the morning. He nearly died when they told him her car had been found abandoned near Villa El Salvador.

That was the state Raquelita found him in when she returned beaming and instead of saying my father's going to kill you, simply beamed at him, switched on all the lights, asked him to sit with her for a while in the living room, and told him he'd die when he heard her news.

'I called the police . . . what happened, Raquelita? What happened to you?'

'Call them again, would you, and tell them your wife is fine? Go on, give them a ring, then come and listen to my news. You'll die when you hear it. You've always laughed at them, haven't you?'

Them meant the scissors, and Joaquín Bermejo nearly did die, tail between his legs and all, when Raquelita started to tell him that the car had broken down in an awful spot, really Joaquín, why don't they bomb those places off the face of the earth, despicable people? The dregs of society. All they could do was stare without lifting a finger while she was busy telling them to do something apart from just standing staring at her like a bunch of idiots. What a country, rife with people like that, Joaquín. Useless good-for-nothings, foul-mouthed even when it came to helping a decent woman like herself. Do you think that any of them so much as lifted a finger? Not one, which meant there was nothing for it but to set off walking along the motorway. Of course, nobody had the nous to stop and offer me a lift either. You should see what a revolting place it is, Joaquín.

'It's a shanty town. Villa El Savador.'

'It's revolting, that's what it is. A blot on the reputation of a city like Lima.'

'But how did you get home, Raquelita?'

'To think of the way you've always laughed at them. Where would I have been without them? But for them, you'd have been lamenting the death of your wife right now. And to think that my poor children . . .'

'But how did you get home, Raquelita?'

'And to think of how you've always laughed at them. Shame on you, Joaquín. I could have lost my life travelling in that bus. It was dreadful, no lights, and people hanging out of all the windows. I don't know how I managed to spot the destination. There was no other answer. It was the only way I could get nearer to home. And can you believe what happened, almost as soon as I climbed aboard? What dreadful people, Joaquín! What a dreadful country! Barely a minute had gone by before someone had stolen my diamond watch. Who else could it have been but that huge black man pressed against me on my left? He must have thought that because I was a decent woman, not one of their kind . . . he must have thought no one would spot anything in the darkness. But as soon as I realized my watch had gone, I said to myself, this is it, Raquelita, your time has come. Nobody could spot anything in that darkness, so I reached calmly into my handbag. I found them at once. And took them out. You can't imagine how splendid they were, Joaquín. I jabbed the man in the ribs with them. I jabbed at him with all my might, Joaquín, and though you've always laughed at my scissors, reckoned I was crazy and could get killed at any minute . . . you who . . . poor fellow! He handed me back my watch straightaway. I told him to put it in my handbag. I spoke as quietly as I could, in case he had accomplices. The coward. Disgusting black man. Cool it lady, he said, but he wasn't fooling me. These people reckon you'll be stupid enough to back off and put away your scissors. That's what he must have reckoned, but I kept them stuck well into his ribs until the moment I got off that bus. Oh, how revolting, Joaquín! Clean them for me, will you? They've got bloodstains all over them.'

'It's incredible, Raquelita. He might have killed you.'

'One of those dregs of society?'

'Let's go to bed, Raquelita.'

'Admit it, you're ashamed of yourself, aren't you, Joaquín? One day you'll learn that as long as I have my scissors with me . . .'

'Let's go to bed, Raquelita.'

'Clean them for me first. Don't forget that tomorrow is another day and that Lima is rife with these people. How revolting! The dregs of society! The absolute dregs! Disinfect them for me, will you?'

Raquelita had fallen asleep, a happy smile on her face at her feat of daring, while Joaquín was still trying to get her to see it from the black man's point of view. He could imagine the man arriving home completely terrified, a gory wound in his side. The world turned upside down. He had tried to explain to Raquelita that the man might have been returning home after an honest day's work. No chance. He was part of the dregs of society. Joaquín had imagined him an honest workman, arriving home somewhere in the back of beyond, imagined his wife and children listening to his story in horrified disbelief. Not a chance. He was part of the dregs of society. Raquelita, I ask your forgiveness for the Scamarone Affair, but you must admit that in this case it was you who was in the wrong. Not a chance. He was part of the dregs of society. And Joaquín had been on the point of saying that when it comes down to it, it's me who is part of the dregs of society, but it was no use. The dregs were that Negro.

Now Raquelita was sleeping the sleep of the just and Joaquín said to himself there's the secret. There. When you don't know, as with the chicken and the egg, you choose. And Raquelita had chosen. That was her secret. And the power of a pair of scissors was almighty. Yes, almighty. Which explained why she had been so unconcerned when they had switched on the bedroom light and discovered her diamond watch had been on the dressing-table all the time.

'Raquelita! Whose watch have you got in your handbag?'

Translated by Nick Caistor

UNITED STATES

The Rites

ROLANDO HINOJOSA

'The hospital? But that's absurd, Ibby. She's pregnant, that's all. She has the baby, and that's the end of it.'

'It isn't that simple, Anna Faye. Graciela says the girl's not strong enough.'

'It's even simpler than that, Ibby: she has her baby and then she goes right back to Nicaragua.'

'Guatemala.'

'One of the two . . .'

'Well, it is Guatemala, and the girl needs to be looked at in town. And she's thirteen . . . And it is Sanford's baby.'

'Stop that.'

'It is.'

'You don't even know that! None of us do.'

'He does.'

'What's there to be excited about, anyway?'

'I'm not excited, I'm calm, but I won't be calm for too goddam long. Listen to me, Anna Faye: I'm the one that's got to see this thing through. Again.'

'Well . . . I . . . I . . . I do too, you know.'

'What you want is to ship her out.'

'Don't you?'

'But not right now. There may be complications.'

'You keep *saying* that.'

'Because it's true; because she's very pregnant, and because she's under fucking age.'

'Ibb-by! Please!'

'Well, she is, goddammit!'

'All right, what do we do?'

'We fix it, but this is the last goddam time! She's a . . . a . . . a kid, for Christ's sake!'

'Ibby!'

'Listen, sister dear, goddammit: Sanford Blanchard has got

149

another maid pregnant. Is that ten, now ? Twenty?'

'We'll take care of her . . .'

'This one needs a hospital; we have to take her in to see Charlie Dean. He may be a piece of absolutely worthless shit, but at least he's a doctor . . . And he's *ours*.'

'Don't be crude, Ibby.'

'I'll crude you, Anna Faye. Face it, goddammit: the girl's *preñada*; fat; *panzona*; knocked up; that fucking way; in trouble; *está pa'parir*; the *works*.'

'You're terrible.'

'Poor damn thing is ugly, ignorant, and illegal. And *we* got her *that way*. In another five months, we chuck her out, fly her out of here, and then twenty a month will feed her and the kid for ever . . .'

'Ibby. You make it sound . . .'

'As if Sandy did something bad, Anna Faye? Is that it? That we're sons-of-bitches, Anna Faye? Well, you're goddam right. *He* did, and *we* are.'

'But what you're saying . . . .'

'What I'm saying is that Charlie Dean will tend to her and then operate on Sandy. You hear me? A vasectomy, Anna Faye; it should've been done years ago.'

'A *what*? But that . . . why, that's terrible.'

'Terrible? We're not talking about some young slick in town here. We're talking about the Klail-Blanchard-Cooke – Ranch! Anna Faye: he's fifty-six years old, goddammit! He's *my* age! Look: we should've done it years ago.'

'You've already said that.'

'Yes, goddammit, I've already said that! You keeping count? Well, that old son-of-a-bitch is populating half of Central goddam America by himself. You keeping count of that, too?'

'Oh, Ibby . . .'

'Where is he now?'

'Ah . . .'

'Well?'

'Out.'

'Anna Faye, Anna Faye . . . *Where* out?'

'To town . . . with Sidney.'

'With Sidney? Marvellous! Simply goddam marvellous!

Now there's a couple of goddam openers for you . . . Just a minute . . . Hold it . . . Who's driving?'

'Evaristo . . . He drove them in early this morning.'

'Evaristo! Evaristo Garcés is a blind man, Anna Faye . . . What are those idiots up to now?'

'I think they were going . . .'

'Say it.'

'To Mexican town.'

'Are – you – sure?'

'No . . . I'm not . . . Please, Ibby . . . I . . . I . . . just thought . . .'

'What? Just what did you think, goddammit? No . . . you listen. No one's coming into this ranch with some goddam *curandera* and her rusty coat hangers, you hear?'

'IBBY!'

'Batshit!'

'Ibby, Evaristo's with them . . .'

'*With* them? Don't you understand, Anna Faye? The man – is legally – blind. Oh, the hell with it . . . Come on, let's go see the girl.'

'She's in the kitchen.'

'She's not working, is she?'

'No! She just sits there, that's all.'

'We'll bring Graciela with us.'

'To Charlie Dean's office?'

'To calm her down . . . Charlie's to meet us at the clinic first. What *is* her name?'

'Nicéfora.'

'Some goddam Guatemalan saint, I'll bet . . . God, when I think of Sanford . . .'

'Sanford needs help, Ibby.'

'Help? You know what he needs? He needs for us to tie a rubber band around his balls so they'll fall off in a week or two.'

'Ibby!'

'Shut up, Anna Faye. The last thing I need is for you to try shit an old turd like me.'

'Do you *enjoy* talking dirty?'

'Do you *enjoy* cleaning up after Sandy? And where is he *now*? Out with *Sid*ney! And, and, and with Evaristo, for God's sake . . . Well, shit, at least there's no danger of any of them coming up pregnant, is there?'

'Really, E. B.'

'Ree-ah-lly, shit, Anna Faye! You've known about this crap for over twenty years . . . And what the hell have *you* ever done about it? Zero! *Really, Ibby*! Bullshit, little sister . . . You've always left it up to Freddie and me to clean up after you and good old *San*ford *Thur*low *Blan*chard himself. Well, no more, Anna Faye. He's a shit, a leech, and a coward. A stinking parasite who's never done one goddam thing for the family . . . Son-of-a-bitch has *never* pulled his own weight! But *this* tears it, goddammit! Twenty years of this shit, Anna Faye! Twenty goddam years . . . Vasectomy, hell!'

'Ibby! Ibb! Please, Ibby . . . you're shaking . . .'

'Vasectomy, hell, Anna Faye! You *hear* me? I'm gonna go cut his goddam pecker off. Is *that* funny?'

'Ibby! You're shaking . . . Sit down, Ibby. Please, please, Ibby.'

'Where the hell are you going?'

'To the kitchen; sit down, Ibby. Please . . . I'm going to get you a glass of water . . . Where do you keep those pills?'

'I don't *need* those pills; I need that son-of-a-bitch out of here!'

'She'll be gone in a few months, Ibby.'

'*She*? Anna Faye, you're not even *close*! Sanford, for Christ's sake, Jesus, Anna Faye!'

'Sit down, Ibby. Please sit down. Please . . . I'll be right back . . .'

Evaristo Garcés, the driver, is a Bank-Ranch Mexican. When he retires (and this will be as soon as Viterbo Longoria dies) Evaristo and Nacha, his wife, will then move from the Ranch to Klail City and on into Viterbo's place. The KBC has always provided for its loyal sons.

Today, though, Evaristo has just run over a dog belonging to a youngster in El Pueblo Mexicano in South Klail, and he's gone over to the youngster's home to explain about the accident.

It's an unpleasant chore, but one that needs to be done. From here, Evaristo will drop off Sanford Blanchard and Sidney Boynton at Chabela Godoy's house.

And (as soon as he settles down) E. B. 'Ibby' Cooke will drive Nicéfora Cruz and Graciela Mata to the offices of Charles M. Dean, MD.

Translated by the author

URUGUAY

The Rest is Lies

EDUARDO GALEANO

1

'I'm leaving on Sunday,' I say. 'There's a direct flight to Barcelona.'

'No,' says Pedro.

'No?'

'On Sunday you – we – are going to Guayaquil. And from there . . .'

I burst out laughing.

'Listen . . .' Pedro says.

'I can't stay another day. I have to . . .'

'Listen, will you?'

2

When I tell Alexandra about the change of plans, she says: 'So you're off to see Adam and Eve.' She draws on her cigarette, then adds: 'That's how I want to die.'

3

A grey day in the Santa Elena peninsula, once known as Zumpa. To the north, not far from here, the world is sliced in half. Here it is the weather that's split in two. Six months every year is sunny; the other six the skies are grey.

We walk across the dusty earth. Thousands of years ago, Pedro explains, all this was covered by the sea. If you dig a bit, you can still uncover shells. But now the south winds have left this an arid plain. The south winds and the oil found underneath. And also the kitchens of Guayaquil, whose ovens consumed all the guiacum woods that until a short while ago, fifty years at most, clothed this desert, and were once used for offerings of incense to the gods. All that's left now are a few squat bushes full of thorns that snatch and keep you there, surrounded by derricks nodding in their search for oil, in the midst of a vast, dusty wilderness.

4

'Here we are,' says Pedro, raising the wooden cover.

They're close to the surface, the two bodies in a shallow hole.

We stare at them. Time goes by.

They're lying in each other's arms. He is face downwards. One of her arms and one of her legs are under his body. One of his hands is on her sex. One leg straddles her.

A heavy stone is crushing the man's head; another lies on the woman's heart. A heavy stone obliterates her sex; another covers his.

I gaze at the woman's head leaning against the man or nestling into him, smiling; how radiant she looks, I say, a look of love.

'A look of terror,' Pedro corrects me. 'She saw the killers. She saw them coming, and lifted her hand. These are the stones they used to kill them.'

I can see her raised arm. Her hand shielding her eyes from any sudden threat or nightmare, while the rest of her body went on sleeping, enfolded in his body.

'See?' Pedro says. 'With this one, they smashed his head in.' He points to the web of fissures where the man's skull was splintered: 'There are no stones this size around here. They were carried a long way just to kill them. Who knows how far they brought them.'

For thousands of years they have lain in each other's arms. Eight thousand years, according to the archaeologists. Long before the time of the shepherds, the farmers. Apparently it was the impermeable clay of the peninsula which preserved their bones.

We stare at them. Time goes by. I can feel the sticky warmth from the colourless sky and the hot earth, feel that this Zumpa peninsula loves its lovers, and has clutched them to it without consuming them.

I feel many other things I can't understand but which make me feel giddy.

5

I feel giddy and naked.

'They're growing and growing.'

'That's just the start. Wait a bit, and you'll see,' Pedro warns me as the car speeds through clouds of dust back to the coast.

I know they'll follow me everywhere.

Magdalena saw them, and howled as we left.

6

'It was a woman who discovered them,' Pedro tells us. 'A woman archaeologist called Karen. They are exactly as she found them, two and a half years ago.'

Above all, I hope no one will disturb them. They've been sleeping in each other's arms for eight thousand years now.

'What will they do there? Build a museum?'

'Something like that,' says Pedro, smiling. 'A museum . . . or perhaps a temple.'

I'm thinking: That hollow is their home, it was untouchable. How many nights are there room for in that long night of theirs?

I wince at the thought of the Lovers of Zumpa Show in the hands of the tour operators: an unforgettable experience, one of the world's great archaeological wonders, snapshots and movie cameras trailed by the swarms of tourists eager to buy thrills. I think back to the lovely shape they make in their embrace, and of all the dirty, unworthy eyes on them. Immediately my face flushes; I'm ashamed at feeling so selfish.

7

We eat at Julio's house on the coast. There's wine, which appears on the table as though by miracle; I know the fish is delicious and the conversation worthwhile, but part of me is elsewhere. Part of me is drinking and eating and listening, and from time to time joins in the talk, but the rest floats up and away, till it is face to face with the bird that's peering in through the window at us. Every lunch-time, the same bird flies down to its branch and observes us all through our meal.

Afterwards, I climb into a hammock, or collapse into one. The sea is whispering its song to me. I open you, uncover you, give birth to you, the sea sings, or through it comes the song of those two, carried from before history, the ones who began our history; the breeze in the leaves takes up the melody. Ancient, familiar airs lift me, enfold me, rock me. Joy, the danger of never reaching an end . . .

'Wake up, sleepyhead!'

I shield my eyes with my hand.

Pedro's sudden call drops me back into the world.

8

'No,' Karen says, 'they weren't killed. The stones were put there afterwards.'

Pedro makes to protest.

'The stones would have rolled off,' Karen the archaeologist insists. 'If they had been thrown at them, they would have rolled off. They would be next to the bodies, not on top of them. They've been carefully placed on the bodies.'

'What about the fractured skull!'

'That happened a long time later. Probably a car or lorry parked on top of them. They were just below the surface when we discovered them. Only very old bones crack like china in that way.'

Pedro looks at her, at a loss. I'd like to ask her how she felt when she first saw them appear, but I feel a fool, so keep quiet.

'Those stones were put there when they were buried, to protect them,' Karen goes on. 'They're part of a cemetery. We found lots of skeletons, not just those of the . . .'

' . . . lovers,' I finish for her.

'Lovers?' she repeats. 'Yes, that's what they're known as. It's a nice idea.'

'But they also found traces of houses,' says Pedro. 'And of food – shellfish and oysters. Perhaps the dead were buried in their homes, like other tribes which . . .'

'Perhaps,' Karen admits. 'There's a lot we still don't know.'

'Or there could be a time difference, couldn't there? A gap of thousands of years between the cemetery and the houses. The lovers might have lived either a long time after or before the other skeletons.'

'Perhaps,' says Karen, 'but I doubt it.'

She serves us coffee, her children chasing a dog in the

background, and explains that it is impossible to disturb the bones after such a long time.

'We left them as they were,' she says, 'so they wouldn't disintegrate. As far as I know they are the first couple buried like this to have been found, which means they've aroused considerable scientific interest. Several osteologists, as we call them, have visited the grave. They confirmed the skeletons were those of a man and a woman, both of them young when they died. Between twenty and twenty-five years old. The ... osteologists say all the skeletons are from the same period.'

'What about carbon-14?' Julio asks. 'Didn't you do those tests as well?'

'We sent other bones from the cemetery to the United States. The carbon-14 tests gave a date of between six and eight thousand years. The bones of the ... lovers can't be analysed, apart from a single tooth we took from the man. Thermoluminescence, and all that. The results were useless. They suggested anything between six and eleven thousand years. If we'd known, we'd have left his teeth in peace.'

Pedro was waiting for this chance. 'Just imagine,' he says in triumph, 'that in many, many years from now, experts use those same methods to analyse the remains of our civilization. They'd find packs of Marlboro in the Coliseum at Rome.'

Amused at the thought, Karen gives a hearty laugh, but later, over our second cup of coffee, she tells us: 'I know you won't like what I'm going to say.'

She gazes at the three of us, weighing us up unhurriedly, then lowering her voice, as though giving a secret verdict, she explains: 'Those two did not die in each other's arms. They were buried like that later on. We don't know why. No one will ever know why they were buried in that position. Perhaps because they were man and wife, but that isn't really a good enough reason. If that were so, why were none of the other couples buried in the same way? It's a mystery. Perhaps they both died at the same time. The bones show no trace of violence. Maybe they drowned. They were out fishing together and drowned. Maybe. For some reason, which we'll never know for sure, they were buried in each other's arms.

They did not die in that position, and they were not killed. It was their grave we found them in, not their house.'

9

We walk among the sand-dunes at nightfall. The sea is shimmering in the distance.

'According to the experts,' Pedro says, 'there could be no such thing as lovers so many thousands of years ago, in a group of semi-nomadic fishermen who had no idea of property, but ... but I think it's nowadays that they are impossible.'

The three of us walk on in silence, staring at the ground.

I'm thinking how enormous they seem, though they're no bigger than us, and how mysterious. More mysterious than the great bird outlines at Nazca, I'm thinking. More of a symbol for me than the cross, I'm thinking. And again: a better monument for America than the Machu Picchu fortress or the pyramids of the Sun and Moon.

'Have you ever seen the body of someone who's drowned?' asks Julio. 'I have. Their bodies are clenched in a position of ... horror; when they're pulled out they're as stiff as boards. If those two had drowned, they couldn't have been forced into that embrace afterwards.'

'What if they didn't drown? There are other ways to die.'

'I don't believe that either,' Julio replies. 'Dead bodies stiffen up quickly. I don't know ...' he hesitates. 'Karen is the expert. She knows, but ... I'm not so sure. I don't think ... they're in such a natural position. No one would have buried them like that. Their embrace looks so real ... what d'you reckon?'

'I believe them,' I reply.

'Who?'

'Those two.'

10

Why won't you two lovers of Zumpa let me find sleep?

I get up in the middle of the night. I go out on to the balcony, take a deep breath, open my arms wide.

I can see them, betrayed by the moon, somewhere in the air or on the ground. I can see the naked figures creeping stealthily up on them through the mangrove swamps, then leaping on them, black stone daggers or sharpened shark bones at the ready. I can see her start with terror, and the blood. Then I see the murderers placing the stones they've carried such a long way on top of the bodies. The first policemen, the first priests of an enemy god put one stone on the man's head, another on the woman's heart, two more stones on their sexes, to prevent any wisp of smoke escaping, that maddening smoke which makes heads spin, which threatens their world – and I smile in the knowledge that no stone can stifle it.

11
The next morning, the way back.

The vegetation increases as I leave the plain behind; a smell of greenery fills the air as I penetrate the moist, luminous world of Guayaquil. Alongside me, now and for ever, are those two who best met death.

Translated by Nick Caistor

Presence

JUAN CARLOS ONETTI

for Luis Rosales

I had spent several days with the dirty money they sent me after the forced sale of the newspaper. For me now there neither was nor would be any Santa María rebuilt, nor *El Liberal*. Everything was dead, reduced to ashes, lost in the river, in nothingness. I ate with friends, got drunk with them, shut myself away for days on end in my flat. And always the filthy money in my pocket, without it ever getting less, without ever spending the least peseta of it. At times I was hungry, or too lazy to go and eat; at others I just watched the hours go by, from the senseless commotion of the dawns to nightfall, lying on my bed, saying my name over and over again syllable by syllable, staring at María José's photograph, which went automatically from pocket to night-table and back again every morning. Only in insomnia could I permit myself to realize that I was not happy and was missing everything. It was only twenty centimetres on my world map from Santa María to Madrid.

Occasionally I received *Presencia*, a news-sheet run off on a badly inked duplicator. It arrived from all the most absurd places in the world, and I used to imagine the unknown group of Sanmarianos taking turns to edit and distribute it. Always bad news. General Cot's tyranny was savage, and whoever was doing this work must have had the vocation of a martyr. And I felt obliged to spend the money from the expropriation on María José, entirely on her.

The man is not exactly small, it's more that life has shrunk him, though still leaving him a huge skull, a greasy sheen on his forehead, a fixed gleam of anxiety in his troubled eyes. Something spider-like about his hands as he lets them drop like objects on the desk, clasps them to put on a show of resolution, to demonstrate to me that he is still alive in spite of all the hardships in the past I imagine for him, in spite of the constant ebbing of hope. He asks questions, ruminates, half-heartedly breaking with cunning, cheating, and his ingrained habit of lies and embellishment. He does not smile, but leans forward, looks at me, then turns his head. He says, feeling his way:

'I'd need five thousand to start organizing things. These matters are always difficult. I've got the perfect man for the job free at the moment. But I can't keep him without work, in reserve. I need five thousand in cash. After that, we'll see.'

I realized I'd found just the companion in madness, in my game, that I had been looking for. I gave another glance at the advertisement:

Private detective – A. Tubor – Castilla Vieja,
30. Madrid and Spain. Discretion.

As I counted out the notes, I smiled at him to show my belief, my timid enthusiasm. He let the money drop on the desk-top, withdrawing his hands with a frown. We were both suspicious. All at once he said in a threatening tone:

'I have to fill in a form.'

As he went towards the cabinet – and in the room, still cold at the start of spring, it was the only piece of furniture apart from the desk itself and two chairs – I realized I had been right, that he had short, weak legs. He came back holding an orange folder, sat down and searched in his pocket for the only ballpoint he had left. He wrote the date, then with bent head, asked:

'Name?'

'Mine or hers?'

'The files and folders are always in the client's name. You are the client.'

'Malabia. Jorge Malabia,' I said.

I added my address, telephone number. I made one up for María José: 37 Sancho Davila Street.

'What is it you want to know?'

'Everything. I want her followed. I want you to tell me exactly what she does, who she is with. She goes out to work. In a public library. In Fernández de Oviedo Street. I can't remember the number. It's the only one in that street, though. It should be in the phone book.'

'Can you give me a description of her? And a photograph.'

I handed over her photograph without feeling at all sad, feeling, rather absurdly, in some way freed.

'She comes up to about my mouth.' I said, standing up. 'Her hair isn't exactly blonde, better put light brown. I can't remember the colour of her eyes: they're green perhaps. But not always. When you have something, give me a call.'

I left, and the banknotes were still lying on the desk. I had told him: María José Lemos, and the name still seemed so perfect, so much her, like a part of her body, or her skin. The name enveloped and revealed her at the same time.

The man calling himself Tubor, private detective, went down to the bar on the corner and asked for a bottle of wine. The barman didn't look at him or even appear to notice him – Tubor hesitated, then put one thousand pesetas on the grimy wetness between them:

'And take for all I owe you,' he said.

Seated at a table, he began to drink, first to relieve his anxiety, then for pleasure, thus embarking on three days of drunkenness. When finally he slept and woke up in his miserable room, he wet his face and the back of his neck in the basin with the flower pattern. Then he searched in his pockets and walked out into the fresh morning air to the church of San Blas. He bought a thick candle in the shop run by the priest opposite the church, and stepped across the threshold into the darkness, heading straight to the left towards the Virgin that had never failed him.

It was a small statue, roughly carved in wood, with large eyes and so poor and squalid looking that it was forced to work miracles to get itself pardoned: Tubor took advantage of it. Kneeling, he said a large number of *Ave Marias*, trying hard to concentrate, trying hard to drum up some faith. He had so often said: I don't believe in God, but I do believe in the Virgin Mary.

When he got cold and bored, he waited for the shadows to fall at the filthy window with a bottle of wine in front of him. By now there were half a dozen of them in the filing cabinet. He waited for night and silence in the building. Then he went down two floors and along the corridor looking for the night-watchman of Westinghouse Inc.

'The typewriter,' he said.

The man rubbed his rough cheek and demanded:

'Five *duros*. It costs five now. I've been thinking, and it's a favour which might turn out very expensive for me.'

'Five,' he said. And gave him the coins.

Now he had an electric typewriter, the latest model in the newspaper adverts.

REPORT 3/2/78-859:

After a great deal of effort I have succeeded in tracing and identifying MJL, who apparently leads a normal life between her home, her work, and a few girl friends whose names I have not so far been able to discover, and which, in my opinion, are unimportant anyway, although I mention the fact for the sake of completeness. Whilst travelling on a no. 12 bus to Cristo Rey . . .

So, for one thousand pesetas a day, I could have María José free from her prison in Santa María; could see her strolling down streets with her friends, down to the promenade in the mist and the weak sunlight with the fishing boats and the frailer ones from the rowing club – not entirely happy because she wasn't with me, was wondering what could have happened to prevent me from writing, or was thinking of my last letter, with its cautious optimism that hinted between the lines at the possibility of our meeting again.

I saw her lively and full of fun, so much younger, she seemed almost child-like, thanks to the skilful lies I had been writing her. I saw her free, silhouetted as she moved swiftly through the places where we had walked together, the shady resting-places we sought out silently to kiss and caress each other. And I could see her walking with her long stride, face wet from the drizzle, towards the street corner where we first met.

This constant happiness spread itself through twenty days. Tubor called and arranged to meet me in a café two blocks from his office. He had a glass of wine in front of him; I did not want anything to drink. I noticed he was nervous, excited over what he was about to reveal. He looked at me with a repulsive mixture of tenderness and fear in his sordid eyes.

'It wasn't something I could put in a letter. You gave me a task, and I always fulfil my obligations. And not for what I make out of it, I can assure you. What I pay out for the agent and in expenses is almost more than what I charge you. But I gave my word.'

He emptied his glass and called for another. I was waiting for his story like a fresh gift, clearing out space in which to receive it, to get full measure from it. He drank a little, lit a cigarette.

'Montera and Bécquer,' he said. 'Does that mean anything to you?'

'No. I hardly ever go to that part of Madrid.'

'OK. You must be about the only one. Well, near Bécquer Street there's a house of assignation. The best, or at least the most expensive, in the area. Now please don't get upset! She was seen going in there on Monday the seventh, at 5.15 p.m. And of course she wasn't alone.'

Taken aback, stupefied, I could only stammer:

'But she works in the library until six o'clock.'

'Oh, come now! Women! As if they can't find some excuse. I'm sorry, but that's what they were born for. To invent excuses, I mean.'

'Did they see who the man was?' I asked.

'Not the first time. It was as quick as a flash. But afterwards yes. He waits for her every evening when she leaves the library. In a green Seat, licence number 4002 M. He is tall, older than yourself, going grey. But very well dressed.

I asked him to find out where they were going to now, if the man had a flat to take her to; I gave him enough money for another week.

That was the first real day of spring. And so the torment began. I bought a bottle of whisky and went up to my flat, smiling back at the porter, pressing the wrong button in the lift. I shut all the windows, undressed without looking at my penis, and lay down on my bed. I disconnected the bell and the telephone. So, as I smoked and drank, without any difficulty I could see María José leaving the library in Santa

María and climbing into the car. They did not kiss, merely exchanged a knowing smile in anticipation of the scenes shortly to follow in the little house in Villa Petrus that the strong, faceless, tireless man had rented or perhaps owned. It was a Swiss-style chalet with red tiles, as cut off from the outside world as my bedroom was at that moment. Perhaps they drew out with caresses the wait for the bed, or perhaps they threw themselves straightaway into each other's arms. In either case, María José would not let herself be undressed. Just as when she was with me, she herself, standing, took off her clothes one by one, smiling slyly at the man, measuring and enjoying his excitement, his impatience. The house was close by a tumbling river, and rays from the setting sun shone through its windows. I knew the window faced west because the chalet they were in was by now identical to the one where I used to meet her. All at once a series of images began, of all that can be done with walls around you, all that we had done as we felt our way, explored, pursued, in our search to invent the other's pleasure. But what before had been limpid, sacred, was now grotesque, bestial. They were discovering impossible unions, couplings that defied all sense: the grey-haired man ever more voracious, María José ever more animal-like and open, her enormous thighs, out of all proportion to her girl's body, revealing deep inside her, asking, begging, degrading the words of love she had so often groaned to me. In the past: never again now.

When I had finished vomiting I got through the rest of the night wandering slowly through the almost deserted streets, where each car, each traffic light, each passer-by helped distract me, to offer me a fleeting moment of diversion and forgetfulness.

This was how April passed, and I felt almost ashamed that my distress, losing its keenness with the wearing away of the days, was gradually diminishing. After the fair at Seville, where all I did was get bored and tired, where I felt taken in by my friends and all the posters, I returned to Madrid and called Tubor up so often I learnt his number by heart. A week later, when the telephone no longer rang, I went to his office in Castilla Vieja, and found it deserted. Nobody could tell me the private detective's new address. I didn't bother to calculate how much the farce had cost me, and slipped back into my indolent sleepwalker's existence.

But at the beginning of May, Tubor called me:

'I've phoned you time and again, but could never get you. Now I've something big for you, really big. I moved office because the other place was a dump. I was ashamed to meet my friends and clients there. I'm in a hurry. I'll be waiting for you tomorrow at Barajas airport at five o'clock. Five in the afternoon, yes – in the cafeteria. You'll have to bring another five thousand. I've almost used up the rest. It's a long time since I've had such a difficult case. Don't forget: if you fail me, everything will fall through.'

I had quite a lot of trouble finding him, making him out among the crowd, the unfriendly stream of those arriving after passing through customs, and the little warmth I felt towards those awaiting their departure, the stuttering voice of the loudspeakers. The same repulsive, battered face, shaved and clean. His clothes seemed completely out of context: they were far too new, a black-and-silver tie stood out against a dazzling white shirt. He'd neglected his shoes, they needed polishing, were a bit out of shape. On the table was a small brown square suitcase, with his initials in gold. It looked like a cash-box.

We shook hands without a word and I handed over the wad of notes. We scarcely spoke because his plane was on the point of leaving. He didn't tell me where he was going, and I didn't care. I can only remember a few phrases and the way he gestured with his hairy hands.

'You won't believe it, but it's true. Proved beyond a doubt. The most difficult investigation I've ever had. Disappeared; the bird's flown. She hasn't gone back to the library; they know nothing of her in her house. As they say: vanished into thin air.'

'The photograph,' I said softly.

'Of course.' He took out a brand new wallet and after some searching placed the photo, now in a plastic cover, carefully on the table.

He was looking round everywhere, as if his aeroplane was in the room and might get away without him. I got up without saying goodbye and went outside to look for a taxi.

A short while afterwards, the furious summer heat descended on Madrid. Three months of hell, people kept saying. One day, in the afternoon delivery, a copy of *Presencia* posted in Switzerland arrived for me. I looked at it without much enthusiasm, unfolded it, and saw in a little box:

María José Lemos, student, held on Latorre island since the military takeover, was taken prisoner by members of the National Guard on 5 April, as she was leaving prison to regain her freedom. She has been missing since that date, and no police or military authority will admit any knowledge of her whereabouts.

Translated by Nick Caistor

The Museum of Vain Endeavours

CRISTINA PERI ROSSI

Every afternoon I go to the Museum of Vain Endeavours. I
ask for the catalogue and I sit down at the big wooden table.
Though the pages of the book are a little smudged I enjoy
poring over them, and I turn them as if I were turning the
leaves of time. There's never anyone else there reading and I
suppose that's why the attendant lavishes so much attention
on me. As I'm one of her few visitors she tends to spoil me.
No doubt she's afraid she'll lose her job because of lack of
public interest. Before going in I always study the printed
notice on the glass door. It says: *Opening hours: Mornings
9.00–2.00. Afternoons: 5.00–8.00. Closed Mondays*. Although I
know which Vain Endeavour I want to look up I still ask for
the catalogue, just to give the girl something to do.

She politely asks me: 'What year do you want?' And I
reply, for example: 'The catalogue for 1922.'

After a moment she reappears with a fat book bound in
purple leather and places it on the table in front of my chair.
She's very kind and if she thinks there's not enough daylight from the window, she herself switches on the bronze
lamp with the green shade and positions it so that its light
falls on the pages of the book. Sometimes when I return the
catalogue I make some brief remark. I might say, for
instance: '1922 was such a busy year. There were a tremendous number of people engaged in Vain Endeavours. How
many volumes do they fill in all?' And she'll tell me very
professionally: 'Fourteen.'

Then I contemplate some of the Vain Endeavours of that
year. I watch children attempting to fly, men set on making
money, complicated machinery that never worked, and
innumerable couples.

'1975 was a much richer year,' she says somewhat glumly.
'We still haven't managed to record all the entries.'

Thinking out loud, I say: 'The classifiers must have an enormous amount of work to do.'

'Oh, yes,' she says. 'Several volumes have already been published and they're only up to the letter C. And that's without the repeats.'

It's really very curious how people repeat Vain Endeavours. However, their subsequent attempts aren't included in the catalogue: they'd take up too much space. One man made seven attempts to fly, each time equipped with different apparatus; several prostitutes wanted to find alternative employment; a woman wanted to paint a picture; someone struggled to lose his sense of fear; almost everyone was trying to be immortal or at least lived as if they were.

The attendant assures me that only a tiny percentage of all the Vain Endeavours undertaken actually get into the museum. Firstly, because the administration doesn't have enough money and it's almost impossible to make purchases or exchanges or get the museum's work known either at home or abroad. Secondly, because the enormous number of Vain Endeavours continually being embarked upon would require an army of staff willing to work with no prospect of recompense or of public sympathy. Sometimes, despairing of official help, they've turned to private sponsorship, but the results have been meagre and discouraging. Virginia – that's the name of the charming attendant I talk to – tells me that these private sources imposed too many conditions and were rather unsympathetic, out of the tune with the aims of the museum.

The building itself is on the outskirts of the city on a piece of waste ground full of cats and rubbish where, just below the surface, one can still turn up cannonballs from a distant war, tarnished sword hilts, or the jawbones of mules corroded by time.

'Have you got a cigarette?' Virginia asks me with an expression that ill conceals her anxiety.

I look in my pockets. I find a rather battered old key, the sharp end of a broken screwdriver, my return bus ticket, a button off my shirt, a few coins and, at last, two crumpled cigarettes. She smokes furtively, hidden amongst the thick broken-spined volumes, the grandfather clock that always shows the wrong hour, usually one just gone, and the dusty old mouldings. They say there used to be a fort on the site where the museum now stands, built in time of war. They made use of the massive stones from its base and some of the beams, and shored up the walls. The museum was inaugurated in 1946. They still have some photographs of the ceremony, with men in tails and ladies in long, dark skirts, paste jewellery and hats decked with birds and flowers. In the background you can make out an orchestra playing chamber music. The guests, captured cutting a cake tied with the official ribbon, look half solemn, half absurd.

I forgot to mention that Virginia has a slight squint. This slight defect lends a comic touch to her face that makes her seem less ingenuous. As if the refraction of her gaze were a stray witty remark, made out of context.

The Vain Endeavours are grouped by letter. When the classifiers run out of letters, they add numbers. This involves long, complicated calculations. Each one has its pigeonhole, folio number and description. Walking amongst them all with that unusual briskness of hers, Virginia could be a priestess, a virgin in some ancient cult, outside time.

Some Vain Endeavours are splendid; others sombre. We don't always agree on their classification.

Leafing through one of the volumes, I came across a man who tried for ten years to get his dog to talk. And another who spent more than twenty years wooing a woman. He brought her flowers, plants, books on butterflies, offered her trips abroad, wrote poems, invented songs, built a house, forgave all her faults, put up with her lovers, and then committed suicide.

'It was a very difficult undertaking,' I say to Virginia. 'But who knows, maybe he found it exciting.'

'Well, it's classified as "sombre",' she replies. 'The museum has a complete description of that woman. She was frivolous, talkative, fickle, lazy and sullen. She was far from tolerant and, what's worse, an egotist.'

Then there are the men who made long journeys in search of non-existent places, irretrievable memories, women who died, and friends who disappeared. There are the children who undertook impossible tasks, full of enthusiasm. Like the ones digging a hole that kept filling with water.

Smoking is not allowed in the museum, neither is singing. The latter prohibition seems to trouble Virginia as much as the former.

'I'd quite like to sing a song every now and then,' she confesses wistfully.

There are people whose Vain Endeavour consisted in trying to reconstruct their family tree, in scratching around in a mine in search of gold, or in writing a book. Others clung to the hope of one day winning the lottery.

'I like the travellers best,' Virginia tells me.

There are whole sections of the museum devoted to their journeys. We reconstruct them through the pages of the books. After a time wandering over different seas, passing through shady woods, discovering cities and markets, crossing bridges, sleeping in trains or on platform benches, they forget the reason for their journey but still continue travelling. One day they just disappear without leaving a trace, not even a memory, lost in some flood, trapped in a subway, or asleep for good in a doorway. No one claims them.

Before, Virginia tells me, there were some private researchers, enthusiasts, who provided material for the museum. She can even remember a time when it was fashionable to collect Vain Endeavour activities as others indulge in philately or embalming specimens.

'I think the sheer number of items put paid to that craze,' says Virginia. 'After all, it's searching for things that are in short supply that's exciting, the possibility of finding something rare.'

In those days they'd come to the museum from all over, they'd ask for information, get interested in a particular case, go away with all the leaflets and come back loaded with stories that they'd write down on the forms, attaching any relevant photographs they'd found. They brought these Vain Endeavours to the museum as if they were bringing butterflies or strange insects. For example, the story of the man who spent five years trying to prevent a war only to have his head blown off by the first mortar shell. Or Lewis Carroll, who spent his life fleeing draughts and died of a cold the one time he went out without his raincoat.

I mentioned, didn't I, that Virginia has a slight squint? I often amuse myself trying to follow her gaze – I can never tell exactly which direction she's looking. When I see her cross the room, weighed down with papers and all kinds of documents, the least I can do is to get up from my chair and go and help her.

Sometimes, halfway through a task, she complains a bit.

'I'm tired of all this coming and going,' she says. 'We'll never get it all classified. There's the newspapers too. They're just full of Vain Endeavours.'

Like the story about the boxer who tried five times to recover his title only to be put out of action by a bad blow to his eye. He probably spends his time in some sleazy part of town mooching from one café to another, recalling the days when his eyes were good and his fists were deadly. Or the story about the trapeze artiste with vertigo who couldn't bear to look down. Or the one about the dwarf who wanted to grow and travelled the world looking for a doctor who could cure him.

When she gets tired of moving the books around Virginia sits down on a pile of dusty, old newspapers, smokes a cigarette – stealthily, because it's not permitted – and reflects out loud, in a tone of resignation:

'I should get another job.'

Or: 'I don't know when they'll pay me this month's wages.'

I tried inviting her to come for a walk in the city with me, to have a coffee or to go to the cinema. But she wasn't keen. She'll only talk to me within the grey, dusty walls of the museum.

I'm so absorbed in what I'm doing in the afternoons I scarcely notice time passing, if it does pass. But Mondays are days of pain and abstinence, when I don't know what to do or how to live.

The museum closes at eight o'clock at night. Virginia herself turns the metal key in the lock, that's as far as her security measures go, after all no one's likely to burgle the place. Though she told me about a man who did break in once with the intention of removing his name from the catalogue. It seems he wanted to erase all trace of some Vain Endeavour he'd embarked on in his youth that he felt ashamed of now.

'We caught him in time,' Virginia says. 'But we had a really tough job dissuading him. He insisted that his endeavour was a purely private matter and wanted it returned to him. On that occasion though, I was a model of firmness and decision. Well, it was a rare piece, almost a collector's item, and it would have been a serious loss to the museum had he succeeded.'

When the museum closes I leave with regret. At first, the thought of the time that has to elapse between then and the next day seemed intolerable to me. But I've learned to wait. And I've got so used to Virginia being there I can't imagine the museum without her. Evidently the Director (he's the one in the photograph with a sash of two colours across his chest) feels the same way, for he's decided to promote her. But, since there's no ladder of promotion established by law or precedent, he's invented a new post, which is in fact the same one under a different title. To emphasize the sacred nature of her mission at the portals of the museum, he has appointed her Vestal of the Temple, to guard the fleeting memory of the living.

Translated by Margaret Jull Costa

VENEZUELA

The Game

LUIS BRITTO GARCÍA

When Cortés presented the Aztec ball game to the court of Carlos V in the year 1528, the deeper meaning of the game naturally remained hidden from the spectators.

Walter Krickenberg *The Ancient Cultures of Mexico*

Do not fall, my lord, do not fall
Because whoever falls
Will never rise again.

Song of the Giants of the First Age

The alien sun rises above the horizon while we are purifying the attributes of our game. Only firm intent and firm binding can assure the perfect balance of breastplates, belts, racquets and helmets. The hieroglyphed shirts which make plain the link between each player and his star are missing, but no matter: this bitter fasting and exercise have all but turned the players into celestial bodies. We are allowed to trace the lines of our rectangle in accordance with the patterns of the sky, though everything in that sky has now changed, apart from the constellations which looked down on us during our obligatory vigil. The rituals have ordained that I am to be the morning star; this morning, I am to return from my voyage through the nether regions, though this violates the sacred harmonies of our calendar; a sign of either discontent at our long journey across the divine waters of the sea, or of the destruction of a world.

While we are dividing up the regions of the sky among us, the pallid spectators appear. As morning star, I come out of the East. I have travelled through the land of the dead, gathering the bones of a new mankind. The players avert their faces so as not to see my polluted light. I am Lord Tlahuizcalpantecuhtli, the bringer of destiny. Who shall I strike first?

Out of the East I launch the ball.

The Sun's blow fells the first player like a headless partridge. It flutters towards the North, the house of darkness. The Sun too attacks the North, home of the dead. Swathed in the white ring of ill omen, the Moon advances to block his progress. Launches at him the skulls of her meteorites. They wound him sorely, striking at him with their necklaces made of human hearts. The Tzontemoque meteorites fall on him, the ones who dive from the skies to bring us caresses or blows. The mother star, with her robe of shells where the stars whirl, rushes out to the attack. Mamalhuaztli too, here known as Orion, joins in against the Sun. Mamalhuaztli strikes him with the three stars drilled in his fist. Tianquiztli, the Pleiades, swarm round him like bees. Colotlixayac, scorpion-faced, lashes the Sun with its tail. Citlallinpopoca, the smoking star, stabs with the rest. Their blows reduce us to darkness.

The Sun falls into Citlacue, the skirt of stars, the sundered tree which splits the fields of the sky. Lady of the starry robe, you who give life to children, will you also be against him? Will you strike him down with your flint, the begetter of the Gods?

Now he burns brightly. Now he is our strength. Now our Lord the Sun flashes like lightning as he rises, shaking off stars. Xiucoatl, the serpent of fire, gleams in his hand. I spin around him; whenever he comes near, I push him on towards his destiny. At each move, a star dies. Our Lord Sun devours his sister Moon. The bat tears the heart from death. We fall like blinded giants through a starless night. The jaguar of darkness devours us.

I aim the ball to the East. In the East the Sun is reborn. He advances to meet the one in the red mask, the one with white plumage, the one who carries the shield and the cudgel. The blows of the combat make blood spurt from our forearms. The Sun tears out the heart of darkness. The blood spurts from our ears. Our blood drives on our Lord Sun.

Are we giants, or stars?

Are we stars, or flowers?

Are we stars who think we are at play?

Musicians dressed in five colours play the five musics of

the five ages. We climb the sky, and beyond each sky is another sky.

We suck the flowers which never wither.

There is no time, no pain, no sadness. We are mists and clouds. Birds and precious stones. What could be more glorious than this springtime? The wind that sweeps it away. I am the bowman, I am destiny. Against the Sun I fling the deadly weapon of the winds.

Like monkeys we flee the storm.

I launch the ball at the South.

We tread azure paths towards the temple built of bones. The thorns of fatigue pluck at us. The sand from the windstorm lacerates our faces. The many-eyed skull peers at us: inside each eye we see the death of every Sun and of every man. Every look inside is a stab of pain.

The bird of death slits our throats.

The Sun is drowned in the rivers of fire. Butterflies and birds make their escape.

We accompany our Lord Sun to the West. To the house of darkness, where the twisted bone of the Moon is reborn.

The long-beaked bird offers him a heart, and blood.

A tree is born of the ocelot-faced Goddess.

The lizard cuts the foot of the Lord of the House of Dawn. The reborn stars fall to earth again, their vessels full of the pulque spilt by the crescent Moon. With pulque we dull the senses of the renascent Sun so he may not flee from the Lord of Shadows. With pulque that leads him astray into the flood of drunkenness. The currents of the fire and water of war are threaded together. We tear off our skin. We are drowned in the flood like fish. The Lord of Shadows descends in the tidal waves of our sweat. The sky falls in.

The four of us who defend the four corners of the earth lift the sky on our shoulders.

With our blows we rekindle the Sun, now no more than the darkness, the wind, the fire and the rain which bring about its death, because to shine out, every Sun must also pass away.

Blinded by the darkness. Swept away by the wind. Charred by the fire. Drowned by the rain.

We have reached the Centre.

As often as we have died we have come to life again.

Stars and men gaze at us motionless.

The corn of days sends forth a single plant. A single mouth devours it.

Like the sun, we pass away and endure.

How to be above life, above the star? And above our own hearts, throbbing as they gaze at men?

Despising them.

To keep the Sun alive, men sacrifice hearts. To keep time alive, we sacrifice Suns to the Gods.

This fifth Sun, the one of our moment, must also die.

With darkness, wind, fire, and rain we strike the Sun. The earth shakes from our combat. The tremor of the blows rattles our bones. I fling him against the tall stem of dripping fire, as though to pierce the sky. I meet him with my body, shudder with the collision, he bounces against the ring of the game's rectangle, and dies.

Blood spurts from my chest. I fall into the Centre.

I have lost the game.

Your whey-faced courtiers rise up, shouting.

I have let the Sun die in the Centre, my Lord Emperor Carlos V. A dead ball rolls to a halt before your throne in the West. Now I too shall die in the Centre, as is the custom. Since I let the Sun die, I must perish with him. Then I shall leave for the house of dawn, and there meet all those warriors who have died in combat or in sacrifice. Their hearts torn from the centre of their breasts.

The players are waiting for you to tear out my heart, you our Sun, Lord Carlos V, as you walk away followed by your courtiers who glitter with the gold stolen from our temples, their shadows as long as the tails of shooting stars.

I step forward to offer my heart to the white priests of the twilight who have come with their knives and their steaming cauldrons to the edge of our rectangle.

I tear off my sacred breastplate as I walk to meet the grimy priests. I proffer my breast, but they pass me by.

They are the cooks, not here to sacrifice us but to share out a pot of leftovers for our dinner, without deigning to look on us.

We eat in darkness, full of tears.

Translated by Nick Caistor

Notes on Authors

ARGENTINA

From the province of Entre Ríos, **Isidoro Blaisten** now lives in Buenos Aires. He has published several books of short stories, including *Felicidad* (1969), *El mago* (1974), *Dublin al sur* (1980), *Cerrado por melancolía* (1982), and *Carroza y reina* (1986).

Daniel Moyano was born in Buenos Aires in 1930. He has been publishing novels and short stories since the 1960s. After the military takeover in Argentina in 1976, Moyano was first imprisoned then went into exile in Spain, where he still lives. His novels include *The Devil's Trill* (1988), *The Flight of the Tiger* and *Libro de navios y borrascas*.

Luisa Valenzuela was born in Argentina in 1938, but now lives mostly in the United States. Her book of stories *Strange Things Happen Here* appeared in 1979, and her novel *The Lizard's Tail* was published in 1983 in the United States and in 1987 in Britain.

BRAZIL

João Ubaldo Ribeiro writes both novels and short stories. He lives in Salvador, Bahía, where he also works as a journalist. He has published *Sergeant Getulio* (1986), and translated his own novel *The History of the Brazilian People*.

Moacyr Scliar is a fifty-one-year-old writer from the south of Brazil. He has published numerous books of short stories and several novels, of which *The Centaur in the Garden* has been translated into English.

CHILE

Born in Chile in 1942, **Isabel Allende** became an international best-seller with her first novel *The House of the Spirits* (1985). This success was repeated with *Of Love and Shadows* (1987). A third novel, *Eva Luna*, was published in 1989. She now lives in Venezuela.

CUBA

Reinaldo Arenas was born in Holguín in 1943. His first novel *Celestino antes del alba* was published in 1967, and his first collection of stories *Con los ojos cerrados* was published in Uruguay in 1970, as Arenas was then in trouble with the Cuban authorities. He spent several years in labour camps during the 1970s, and left with the mass exodus of Cubans in 1980. His novel *Farewell to the Sea* was published in the United States in 1986.

GUATEMALA

Arturo Arias was born in Guatemala City in 1950. He left his native country in 1980 because of the political repression, and now lives in Mexico City. He has written two novels *Despues de las bombas* (1979) and *Itzam Na* (1981).

Rodrigo Rey Rosa's first collection of short stories, *The Beggar's Knife*, was published in 1988.

MEXICO

Jesús Gardea trained as a dentist before turning to writing. Born in Chihuahua in 1939, he has written several collections of short stories, including *Los viemes de Lautaro* (1979) and *Septiembre y los otros días* (1980).

María Luisa Puga has written several books of short stories, including *Cuando el aire es azul* (1980), *Accidentes* (1982), the novels *Parico o Peligro* (1983) and *La forma del silencio* (1987). She was born and lives in Mexico City.

NICARAGUA

Sergio Ramírez is vice-president in the Sandinista government. He has written several novels, of which *To Bury Our Fathers* (1985) has been translated into English. His latest novel, *Divine Punishment*, will appear in English in 1990.

Fernando Silva is a doctor, poet, and short-story writer. His stories of life in the interior of Nicaragua have been collected in *Cuentos*, published by Editorial Nueva Nicaragua in 1985.

PARAGUAY

Helio Vera lives and works in Asunción, the capital of Paraguay.

PERU

Alfredo Bryce Echenique is the author of the novels *Un mundo para Julius* (1970) and *La vida exagerada de Martín Romana*, but is perhaps better known as a short-story writer. Born in Lima in 1939, he lived and worked for many years in France before returning to live in Peru.

UNITED STATES

Chicano writer **Rolando Hinojosa** won the 1976 Cuban Casa de las Américas prize for his novel *Klail City y sus alrededores*, one of a series of novels in which he writes about a small, imaginary US border town.

URUGUAY

Eduardo Galeano writes short stories and essays. His *The Open Veins of Latin America* (1971) was an influential critical history of Latin America; he has since written the trilogy *Memory of Fire*. After living almost a decade in exile in Spain, he has now returned to Montevideo, where he was born in 1939.

Juan Carlos Onetti was born in Montevideo in 1909. His short novels and stories have long been highly regarded throughout Latin America. *The Shipyard* was translated into English in 1961.

Cristina Peri Rossi published her first book of stories in 1963. She left Uruguay for Spain in 1972, and as well as several collections of short stories has written poems and three novels, of which *Ship of Fools* was published in English in 1989.

VENEZUELA

Luis Britto García is from Caracas, where he was born in 1940. He studied law, but published a first book of stories *Fugitivos* in 1964. He became well known in Venezuela when in 1970 he published his first novel *Vela de armas* and a short-story collection *Rajatabla*. For several years he wrote mainly for the theatre, but in 1980 published his most ambitious work to date, a lengthy novel *Abrapalabra*.

steve kleen

1 800 792 5577